The Confession of Hilary Durwood

Also by Euron Griffith

Miriam, Daniel and Me

"a confidently crafted novel about time, change and enduring love"
– Ed Thomas

"I loved how the flashbacks pieced together the backstories of the characters... the historical facts lent authenticity to the story giving a real feel of life in North Wales at that time... I found it engrossing." – c.isfor.claire_reads

"Griffith successfully opens a window on North Wales in the sixties and the life, politics and people of that time"
– @shh_reads_

The Confession of Hilary Durwood

Euron Griffith

Seren is the book imprint of
Poetry Wales Press Ltd.
Suite 6, 4 Derwen Road, Bridgend, Wales, CF31 1LH

www.serenbooks.com
facebook.com/SerenBooks
twitter@SerenBooks

The right of Euron Griffith to be identified as
the author of this work has been asserted in accordance
with the Copyright, Designs and Patents Act, 1988.

© Euron Griffith, 2023

ISBN: 9781781726983
Ebook: 9781781726990

A CIP record for this title is available from the British Library.

The publisher acknowledges the financial assistance of the Books Council of
Wales.

Printed in Bembo by Severn, Gloucester

*This is a novel set in the Victorian era. For authenticity the characters
reflect values of the time relating to British imperialism, social hierarchy,
the position of women, and similar social prejudices.*

To Jacci

Most wretched men
Are cradled into poetry by wrong,
They learn in suffering what they teach in song.

Percy Bysshe Shelley

I HAVE DONE unspeakable things. My conscience is racked by my past deeds and their consequences. Dear Tobias Gently, innocent and trusting, I was the very Devil and led you to your doom. If it is any consolation – and I can hardly believe that it is – your face haunts me in my nightmares and, since that deceitful act on the island, your features have been my constant companion – occasionally appearing in a crowd, or a tavern and now, in my solitude, on the polished surfaces of these stones which surround me in my cell. If I could see you again in tangible, human form I would fall to my knees and cry for your forgiveness but it is too late for now you are probably a ghost hovering over a pile of your own bones beneath that dreadful tower.

The lithe, silver-haired fisherman who rescued me from certain death and took me to the island was also a victim. I may have given him the holy word as a mark of my gratitude but what good was that when I took away the very air he breathed and all that he had ever seen or heard? It is undisputable that the poor fellow – along with his friends – had devilish designs upon my flesh for I fully believed what Mr Samuel Burgess told me about what had happened to his former crewmates aboard the *Great Plains* but, in time, surely he would have repented and rejected his heathen habits? I released his soul prematurely and left it to fend for itself in the tumultuous pit of Purgatory.

Had my crimes terminated here then I would still be deserving of the gallows – but they continued.

The eminent Sir Duncan Roseberry may have tricked me at the cursed tower but he did not deserve his horrendous and gruesome fate. Neither did Mr Eustace Skate – a scoundrel and a cheat for certain – but I shall always try to remember him as a man even more enslaved than myself to the fickle vanities of fame and glory. His face too haunts me nightly as it last appeared to me on that night in London bearing a glazed and shocked expression whilst the monster ripped apart what was left of his earthly form. I did nothing to help even though I was in a position to do so. The demon which tore at his flesh was almost a part of me.

Father, at Havemore Hall, try to forgive your wayward son. The authorities kindly allowed me paper and ink and I wrote frantically and without revision – day and night – in an effort to reach a meaningful conclusion. Not a plea of innocence or for the appliance of mercy but more a confession and the acceptance of my fate.

Now it is done and my hurried effort lies before me in an untidy pile. Your beloved Milton may have attempted to justify the ways of God to Man but, father, I saw my task as being the very opposite and I hope both you and the Almighty will look more kindly upon me after reading my account. I have neither embellished nor lied. Admittedly my prose is occasionally too florid but it is a fault that has regularly been noted by yourself and by masters and tutors alike! Given more time I would have amended and improved. Please try to overlook this shortcoming father and also the greater human failings in your son. My only comfort is that I also inspired great love and loyalty on my adventures – most notably in the heart of Mr Delphus of Clare. A most remarkable creature. Without his dedication and devotion I would not be sitting in this cell tonight watching my breath rise up in fleeting clouds as the rest of London's population sleeps – impatient for the morning when it will gather in Newgate to watch me hang.

Arrival

1. My tale begins with a discourse regarding the mysterious disappearance of Sir Duncan Roseberry.

IT HAD BEEN Mr Eustace Skate who had told me about the Tower of Ectha whilst we dined as guests of the Governor at the long room of the Empire Club in Singapore. Naturally, Mr Skate was a much more experienced traveller than myself, and, like half of my contemporaries at Kings, I'd admired the two memorable and deservedly celebrated volumes he had issued documenting his sailing adventures in the South Seas. Since coming down from Cambridge with a poor degree in Literae Humaniores I had established a modest foothold as an assistant printer with his publisher – the estimable firm of Colebridge and Sons of Piccadilly – thanks in no small measure to the fact that Mr Julius Colebridge himself had once been a Colleger with my father. Mr Colebridge's regard for my father must have been of the highest order for, soon – less than a month into my apprenticeship in fact – he called me up to his office and, aware of my literary ambitions, suggested that Mr Skate and myself should embark on a joint Pacific odyssey and produce a shared volume of our adventures and impressions of some of the lesser-known islands of the Pacific South Seas.

Imagine my joy!

It was a bold and inspired plan on Mr Colebridge's part and one that I'd grasped with indecorous haste but, that evening at the Long Room of the Empire Club, his fine brain addled by the treacherous potency of the 1802 Terrantez Oscar Acciaioly which the knowledgeable sommelier had so effusively recommended – Mr Skate confessed to me that he'd only agreed to our escapade under duress since he had debts he needed to clear at the Athenaeum and Mr Colebridge had placed him under said moral contract as a result of an emancipating sum of money! Despite such a revelation however, it was pleasing to me that Mr Skate had no specific personal animosity towards myself. Indeed, I suspected that he secretly enjoyed the attentions of an eager young writer who invested his career with more respect and reverence than he had previously enjoyed from the public and journalists alike.

Despite my extreme enthusiasm however, Mr Skate soon developed a rather puzzling and near-evangelical urge for solitude. I would knock on the door of his rooms and call his name softly in the hope of learning more of his past travels and adventures but was greeted with nothing but silence broken occasionally by rather dramatic snoring. He would only re-convene with me during the evenings at the Long Room. And it was on one such evening, as we ordered a delectable and potent Madeira from the helpful sommelier that Mr Eustace Skate shrugged off his characteristic reticence for a moment and – having first glanced over his shoulder to assure himself of the sommelier's departure – leant forwards and told me, in hushed and slightly slurred tones, of the mysterious Tower.

Mr Skate described a spectacle which rivalled the Great Pyramids in respect of age, if not dimensions then in antiquity and grandeur, but admitted that these descriptions were primarily based on hearsay and myth since he had not encountered engravings or sketches and that the primary source of his news regarding the Tower was the correspondence he'd entertained with the celebrated explorer and Fellow of the Royal Observatory Sir Duncan Roseberry. Naturally, at the knowledge that Mr Skate was an intimate of Sir Duncan, the excellent vintage Madeira was immediately halted in its progress towards my lips and the glass returned somewhat forcefully onto the mahogany table which separated us.

"Sir Duncan," I whispered in awe.

"Ah," said Mr Skate, with a sad smile and a hint of irony. "You are familiar with the gentleman's name I see?"

"Indeed I am sir," I replied, sitting forwards with renewed enthusiasm. "As, no doubt, is the whole of the empire! Sir Duncan Roseberry is, justifiably, the most celebrated explorer and journalist of our time. Why, his excellent study of the people of the Huripoor and his terrifying account of the excruciating practices of their initiating ceremonies has been a companion of mine on many a long journey. In fact the volume is now in need of re-binding as a result of my repeated consumption."

Mr Skate smiled again.

"It is a fine work," he said, lifting the Madeira casually to his lips, "of that there is no dispute."

I recalled the portrait of Sir Duncan which had graced the wall of the ancient Refectory at Kings. Even though it was over a thousand miles away in distant, verdant Cambridgeshire I was nevertheless able to re-paint the picture stroke by stroke onto the eager canvas of my memory. My mind's brush delineated the piercing blue eyes which – it was said – had broken female hearts from the grand ballrooms of Brighton through to the crumbling caves of Ranthsamoor. It also defined the tumbling blond locks and the trimmed beard and the curious outline of a birthmark in the guise of an Arabian scimitar faintly visible on his forehead. I sighed as I re-lived chilly winter evenings dining with my fellow gentlemen in the full glare of Sir Duncan Roseberry's portrait – his silent but almost accusatory demeanour a daily reminder of greatness and, by comparison, of my wretched unworthiness in harbouring similar ambitions of glory.

"Tell me Mr Skate," I said. "What is the latest concerning Sir Duncan Roseberry? Has he been...?"

Mr Skate looked up to meet my gaze.

"Found?" he offered.

"Yes," I replied, cursing the Madeira for loosening my tongue so effectively. "Naturally I am eager for news, as is the whole of England. I'm told *The Times* has now a regular correspondent devoted to the subject of his disappearance. Even our sagacious Queen has apparently been heard to voice her concern."

Mr Skate sighed deeply and stirred his glass.

"Alas," he said. "I have had no correspondence with Sir Duncan Roseberry for many months. I am beginning to wonder whether it shall ever be continued. I believe that Sir Duncan's purpose in his last journey to the east was to discover the very Tower of Ectha which I spoke of just now. Sir Duncan was always very shrewd and he cloaked his mission in secrecy and now, after such a long period of silence from the great man, it would appear as if we will never hear if he was successful in his quest or not."

Mr Skate stirred his glass one final time before downing the Madeira in one gulp.

"But, of course, as you will know," he said. "Such is the nature of the explorer's lot. If safety and security is your ambition in life then you, I – and I daresay the estimable Sir Duncan Roseberry himself – would have no doubt chosen the life of a simple gentleman farmer."

2. An unwelcome communication invokes a strong desire for revenge.

I SHOULD NOT have been too taken aback when I woke up to find that Mr Eustace Skate had disappeared in the night. A small envelope was discreetly slipped into my hand by the young waiter in the Breakfast Room and, at once, I recognized my own name delineated in Mr Skate's highly individual looped writing. I thanked the young waiter and he bowed and retired – a few coins the richer for his errand.

In truth, my humour was somewhat diminished as a result of the previous evening's anacreontic consumption of the Madeira and I resisted the temptation to open the envelope until I had attempted to rejuvenate my spirits with two fried kippers and a cup of strong coffee. Only thereafter did I pick up the knife and slit the envelope's spine with a swift surgical motion.

Dearest Hilary,

I trust you will forgive my impetuosity but it should be evident to you by now that I have fled Singapore and will shortly be on board a speeding clipper bound for the shores of Siam where I intend to spend a few weeks locating the medieval monastery at Pan Reng. I am informed that it is a perilous trail and I feel that I must implore you not to risk your life in pursuing me. I promised Sir Julius that I should guarantee your physical and spiritual safekeeping and I urge you to regard this warning not as a challenge but as an expression of my pledge to that honoured Man of Letters. Perhaps we shall meet up again in the spring at the Athenaeum when I plan to return to London? I shall, as is appropriate, communicate the sad news of the termination of our joint volume to Sir Julius and, naturally,

I shall absolve you, dear Hilary, of all responsibility and of all our hotel expenses, which I shall honour this day with an express telegram to the offices of Colebridge and Sons in Albemarle Street. Please forgive me.
   Your friend
   Eustace.

Disappointment at the sudden demise of our proposed joint volume was – I am ashamed to report – my initial response to Mr Skate's confession but my second was one of anger. By fleeing during the night like a common thief, Mr Eustace Skate had not only reneged on the terms of his original contract with Sir Julius Colebridge but he had also – regardless of his unconvincing protestations – neglected his promise to Sir Julius and my father to safeguard my physical and spiritual well-being for I was now stranded and friendless in the vice-ridden port of Singapore with only a few jangling guineas between myself and penury.

However, as I stirred the cracked molasses into my coffee, this fury gradually subsided and I wondered whether Mr Skate had not, circuitously and unintentionally, done me a great service. For, as he himself had argued during the previous evening, was it not an explorer's vocation to eschew comfort and to challenge himself against the unknown stripped of all worldly luxuries? Instead of cursing his cheating soul, should I not be *thanking* Mr Skate for this unexpected opportunity? As the sweet coffee soothed my stomach I concluded that the best means of revenge against Mr Eustace Skate's actions lay not in anger but rather in exceeding him in reputation and by continuing to do so until eventually – if it were not too vain a wish – I could even challenge the eminent position of that missing giant Sir Duncan Roseberry himself.

My plan was simple but audacious. I would travel to Siam and discover the monastery of Pan Ren *before* him. Admonished and shamed thus, Mr Eustace Skate would surely rue the day he abandoned his young ward in such a cowardly manner!

Driven by this restless urge for recompense I returned to my rooms, gathered my meagre possessions, substituted the essentials from my old Eton trunk into a hemp sack for ease of transportation, hailed a speeding rickshaw down to the harbour, and, once there, quickly secured the services of a fit and honest-looking young *backoor* (or 'harbourman') who, in return for two of my precious guineas, assured me he could – in three days – deliver me to the shores of Siam and, as Providence would have it, to a little-known inlet a mere few miles from the very village of Pan Reng itself! This fellow – who informed me in his Pidgin English and with a clammy handshake that his given name was Lai Ming – greedily pocketed my coins and I carefully climbed aboard his tiny craft. I tried to ignore its rather ragged nature and settled myself somewhat painfully in the cramped, canvas-walled cabin at the stern alongside a menagerie that included a caged macaw suspended from a somewhat expedient hook and a curled giant centipede in a basket. Lai Ming explained in a rather oleaginous fashion that, in his culture, macaws and giant centipedes were invested with inexhaustible revenues of good fortune and had the added benefit of keeping evil spirits at bay. Both creatures were conveniently caged and were therefore considerably less bothersome and offensive to me than a scuffed and flea-infested mongrel whose domain on this particular vessel I had, in his view, clearly invaded by occupying the cushion at the rear of the craft and who now only surrendered his throne when beaten off by Lai Ming's swishing cane! The abominable mongrel and I became instant enemies and – as the tiny craft was guided out of the harbour by Lai Ming's bamboo oars – this hound assured me of his animosity by the unfettered exhibition of his teeth.

But this animal's lack of grace was of limited concern to me as I gazed out at the passing hulls of anchored junks and as I listened to the laughter of the sailors as they stared down at us and waved (making sinking motions with their hands which seemed to engender much boisterous jollity among their clan). I only thought of Mr Eustace Skate and of how – armed with the advantageous intelligence of Lai Ming's secret inlet – I would beat him to Pan Reng and to the medieval monastery.

I lay back against the bamboo wall of my cabin and smiled as I envisaged the raging success of my account of its discovery whilst Mr Eustace Skate floundered impotently on the waves of the South Seas.

3. A most bizarre evacuation is swiftly followed by a sobering realization.

SUSPICIONS REGARDING THE seaworthiness of Lai Ming's craft were reinforced as soon as we departed the sheltered waters of Singapore harbour and entered the open ocean. The hilly green swells rose up and I sat tight within the confines of the cotton-lined cabin as the canvas walls flapped. My canine tormentor seemed untroubled and greeted my fleeting glances in his direction with Mephistophelean growls. As each wave rolled heavily against us, I felt the palm trunks of the raft separate and creak. I began to understand why the sailors in the harbour had been so amused because the sorry vessel was clearly held together by faith as much as by hemp rope and bindweed. Through the intermittent gaps in the canvas doorway I looked up at Lai Ming as he fearlessly plunged the long, hand-hewn oar into the waves. I tried to communicate my concern with a series of uncomfortable smiles, but he misinterpreted my expression as being borne of contentment rather than terror and responded by raising his free hand and grinning as if the journey was no more eventful than a jaunt along the Cam on a breezy June afternoon! I resolved, rather hopefully, that the valiant buccaneer was, in all probability, blessed with an intuitive knowledge of the ocean and its fickle temperament and that he was also in likely possession of a nearby haven – a cove or palm-lined harbour perhaps – where we could ride out the looming tempest.

However, as the ocean waves redoubled in their green-veined virulence – and as the clouds above us transmuted into eerie fast-moving smoke – the genuine reason for Lai Ming's insouciance quickly became clear. Uttering a sudden and sharply toned command he hailed my Mephistophelean tormentor to his side. Lai Ming scooped the obedient mongrel up in his arms and tossed him into the ocean! Naturally, as an Englishman with a finely developed sense of justice and fair play, I was outraged at such casual cruelty. I struggled to my feet with every intention of protesting my objection for – incompatible as we had been as travelling companions – the poor dog deserved a more fitting reward for his loyalty than such an ignominious end! But before I could stand up to deliver my tirade Lai Ming tightened his purse around his waist, casually released his guiding oar into the possession of the sea and – following a hearty gesture in my direction – he too plunged into the vertiginous depths leaving me stranded and without an oar on the fragile boat!

The waves rolled and the skies turned black. I stepped forwards carefully, clinging on to whatever pole I could find for balance, and watched Lai Ming and his despicable companion negotiating the ocean's obstacles as effortlessly as marine creatures blessed with gills instead of air-sucking lungs. It occurred to me in an instant that this was a well-practiced ruse and that the agreed two guineas fare from innocent and unsuspecting travellers had, over the years of Lai Ming's nefarious trade, ensured that he now had unmatchable swimming skills – together, of course, with a veritable forest of cheap palm logs and an illimitable supply of bindweed.

4. An indelicate predicament.

A FEW MINUTES after Lai Ming and his ragged partner had made good their escape the rain spattered the canvas walls of my cabin like musket fire. The wind increased in tenacity and violence. One petulant and mighty gust was enough to dislodge the cage of the hapless macaw and send him hurtling into an oncoming wave. The same gust which erased this ill-starred animal from all earthly records was kinder to the giant centipede for that individual's basket was merely tipped onto its side therefore allowing the slinky beast to pour himself onto my lap. I had never before been host to such a gargantuan insect and the peculiarity of the situation was not lost on the giant centipede either because he immediately sought a more secluded sanctuary within my breeches. As the spindly limbs of the fiend felt their way along the naked flesh of my inner thigh I followed the course of the moving bulge with trepidation for I had heard Mr Eustace Skate recounting on many occasions how a single bite from this scoundrel could reduce a man to pitiful paroxysms of agony. Intent on evicting the noxious arthropod I once more rose to my feet and – struggling to maintain my balance – I undid the buttons of my breeches and unpeeled them as delicately as was possible over my boots. I gathered the breeches in my arms and sacrificed them to the insolent snatch of the gale. They kicked and flapped their empty legs in protest but were swiftly sucked into the bottomless pit of the ocean. Any discomfort I may have felt at my indecorous state was tempered by the knowledge that I had at least exorcised the giant centipede.

But, upon sitting down again, I discovered that the cunning beast had not, after all, been consigned to the murky depths of the sea but had, instead, curled itself around my groin like a chain and was now tightening its grip by the second! He appeared to find my groin a rather agreeable spot to rest for, although both strands of his antennae would occasionally wave eerily to taste the salt air, the main body of the segmented monster resisted the urge to scuttle off into some caliginous region of the boat and he merely contracted his anatomy even further to consolidate his occupancy.

I was exhausted but unable to sleep. For how was it possible to sleep when the merest motion would aggravate the giant centipede and force him to sink his deadly incisors into the most delicate part of my flesh? I sat there for what seemed like centuries, rocking forwards and back in response to the storm, my limbs paralysed whilst the moon peeped down upon these curious travellers from behind a shifting veil of diaphanous clouds.

Yet, despite my predicament I must have slept for the next thing I remember were my eyes flickering tentatively at the first stabs of dawn. At first I was confused and imagined myself back in my warm room at Holborn but, remembering that I was stranded on the South Seas I jolted forwards and discovered to my amazement that Lai Ming's loosely crafted vessel had somehow survived the worst of the night's onslaught. I then remembered the giant centipede and I glanced urgently at my groin in full anticipation of witnessing his green embrace. But he had vanished! I was finally able to outstretch my limbs and, standing up somewhat gingerly, I closed my eyes, joined my hands together in prayer and thanked the Lord for soothing the ocean and for ridding me of my tormentor!

But, upon opening my eyes, I saw that, although the once turbulent waters were now placid, I was drifting along the ocean currents and trapped in the middle of a barren and watery desert. Hunger clawed like a cat in the pit of my stomach and I scoured the contents of my hastily packed hemp sack for any scrap to eat but it became clear that my haste in leaving Singapore had been most inopportune because, although I had possessed the soundness of mind to pack a few items of light attire – together with a Bible, razor and other miscellaneous articles of a gentleman's toilet – I had completely neglected to include any food. I stood up and studied the horizon, shielding my eyes from the glare of the sun but all I could see was a clinical line – a stark demarcation of sea and sky completely undisturbed by the tip of a mountain or the hazy bulge of land. The realization that I was marooned on the open ocean without food or any visible suggestion of civilization forced me to sink down once more onto the wet pine logs of the raft. I knew that the ocean, for all its present benignity as it lapped playfully against the sides of the craft, was cunning and deceptive for it would surely soon claim my body as mercilessly as it had claimed countless others since the dawn of mankind.

5. How a moment of repentance was miraculously rewarded.

SLUMPED, MAROONED AND trouser-less in the canvas-lined cabin of Lai Ming's boat I was soon distressed by delirious fantasies concerning any form of nourishment but as I surveyed the unending ripples all around me – stretching hundreds of miles in all directions – I began to wonder whether this part of the ocean was host to any form of life at all. Gazing over the side of the log boat I attempted to perceive the faintest suggestion of movement beneath the waves – a fish of some variety, or an edible crustacean – but my eyes were continually repulsed by the shattered reflection of the sun which lay scattered upon the surface of the water like a thousand shards of broken glass. The proximity of my own death provoked an urgent search through the discarded contents of my sack once again. Not for food this time but for the sanctuary of my Bible. The Last Judgement was swiftly approaching, and I was eager to appeal against the Almighty's inevitable verdict that I had been a vain and weak soul. Perhaps I might be granted a period in Purgatory instead of the devilish canyons of Hell?

I clutched the small, leather-bound Bible to my chest and uttered the Lord's Prayer as forcefully as I could but my attention was suddenly diverted by a sound at the far end of boat – a slight scratching barely audible above the lapping of the sea. I placed the Bible down on my lap and focused on the gap between two of the pine logs at the bow of the craft where now two spindly antennae were emerging, sniffing the air, feeling for food or the threat of any immediate predators.

"The Lord Will Provide!" I uttered, smiling as I observed the giant centipede slithering out of his most recent hiding place.

I approached him as gently as I could, licking my lips in anticipation – tightening my grip on the Holy Book and raising it to the skies. But as I raised the Bible in preparation to deal the wretch a lethal blow, my progress was halted by a jolt of compassion. Had not the teachings of the Good Book proclaimed the sanctity of all life – even that of a detestable crawling beast of the jungle? Whilst the giant centipede had caused me undeniable agitation by entwining itself around the delicate and intimate portions of my body had his only crime been that of seeking to find the warmest spot for which to rest during a fierce tempest?

I dropped the Holy Bible to my side and closed my eyes momentarily to wish myself free from this predicament but I was immediately overwhelmed by a sudden stab of excruciating agony. Looking down, I beheld that the giant centipede had rewarded my merciful actions by digging his toxic fangs as deeply as he could into my ankle. The pain was beyond the measure of any discomfort I had ever previously experienced and, within seconds, I was engulfed by an almost unbearable sensation of boiling heat! I screamed and yelled for help, but I knew it was to no avail since some apocalyptic disaster had clearly befallen the civilised world in my absence and now I was the only human being left on the globe! The centipede burrowed even deeper into my leg – whipping his body in paroxysms of greedy delirium as my blood spurted out in a fountain onto the palm logs. I attempted to kick the animal away with my free leg but this manoeuvre was hampered by the numbness which was now enveloping me. I became dizzy. The huge sky above me began to revolve like a fairground carousel. I stumbled, held out my hand for support but found only thin air. My body was being burned alive from the inside. Despite my best judgement I tried to kick the insect away again but stumbled a second time and, this time, I failed to regain my equilibrium for I slipped on the wet pine logs and, in an instant, the burning pain was doused by the icy balm of the ocean as I tumbled headlong into its blue and murky depths, my arms flailing as quickly as they could– the giant centipede still clinging on, still infusing me with its toxic venom as curious fish collided with us, sweeping mad shoals below us, above and all around.

6. Death in the depths of the ocean.

SWIRLING AROUND HELPLESSLY in the icy blueness of the ocean I observed the sunlight spearing in like long, elegant maypoles above me. I sank as swiftly as a Spanish cannon and the water grew darker and chillier. The seabed lay hundreds, possibly even thousands, of feet below me in a domain as alien and as lifeless as the surface of the moon. I imagined my body lying there, pecked and consumed by curious fish until it was reduced to a stark cluster of bones – my bobbing skull grinning ironically at the bizarre location of my final resting place. I envisaged my remains being gradually enshrouded by underwater moss until they were indistinguishable from all the other features of the ocean floor and until there was no possible indication that they had once been the rigid and divinely crafted framework of a man. My lungs were at the extreme edges of their endurance and I sensed the moment approaching when I should finally submit to the inevitable and suck the seductive ocean into my body. At that precise moment would my father – thousands of miles away in England – experience a ghostly shiver as he sat in his study at Havemore Hall? Taking off his spectacles, would he stand up and ring the bell in order to enquire of Molly whether there had been any messenger boys that morning? I would never see Havemore Hall again or run through the maze – teasing Old Jacob as he tended to the hedges, my pockets bursting with apples. If I could have spoken at that moment, I would have said goodbye to the old house. Goodbye to England. Goodbye to family and friends, to all my literary ambitions and to my dreams of encountering strange new lands. I would also have bidden farewell to my dark desire for revenge against Mr Eustace Skate – indeed, as I prepared to inhale the cold and ever-darkening brine and end my life in complete misery and obscurity I forgave him for his misdemeanour and wished him well in his hunt for the monastery at Pan Reng. I was done with this world – my lack of achievement or celebrity within the brief period of my tenancy was now of no consequence. In the enveloping darkness I now saw Death as he swam around me, waiting to claim me and drag me down. *'One breath,'* he seemed to say. *'Take one breath!'*

But then – just as he was upon me – I was suddenly pushed upwards towards the light, past the shimmering maypoles once more, out into the sunlight and the vast profusion of life-giving air.

7. *My condition engenders concern and I impart a most valuable gift.*

THREE STRONG FELLOWS winched me up and laid me out on the deck of their boat. A fourth joined their curious company and, even though the sun was directly behind him I identified him immediately as the one who had risked his life to plumb the treacherous depths to save my soul. Like his companions, somewhat curiously, he had long, thick silver hair which caught the sunlight occasionally like a freshly minted shilling. Naked from his waist up, the muscles on his upper body were as tight as coils of rope whilst his skin glowed like polished marble. The four men were slapping each other on the back in clear mutual congratulation and chattering excitedly in a language that was completely alien to me. Perhaps it was Rotuman- or possibly even the semi-mythical Lauan? I had drifted helplessly for a considerable distance since the storm and, having shamefully neglected to a compass or map, I had only the vaguest approximation of my position. I was somewhere in the Pacific, that much was plain, south of Singapore perhaps? Or possibly east? The only certainty was that I was comprehensively and conclusively lost.

I gathered my strength and sat up, smiling at my new companions in the hope of expressing both gratitude and unthreatening intentions. The youngest of them – the one whom I surmised (by his wetness) had dived down into the depths to save me – responded by immediately producing a skin-bottle full of icy water. He knelt and raised it to my lips. I gulped at this nectar in a most indelicate fashion before returning the bottle and wiping my mouth.

"I'm in your debt my friend," I said, extending my hand.

But the young man did not accept the invitation to shake it. Indeed, at the sound of my words the smile vanished from his face in an instant. I feared that perhaps I had inadvertently uttered a word or a phrase – or offered a gesture – which was somehow offensive to his society. This fear was aggravated when I noted that each of his silver-haired friends had lost their congenial demeanours too and had expressions on their faces which I could only describe as being ones of abject horror and repulsion!

"What is it?" I enquired. "Have I offended you?"

It was then that I observed that the four men were directing their alarmed stares at the lower part of my leg. Looking down I saw that the giant centipede was still attached to my ankle though his whipping motions had now been stilled. My rescuer crouched down and flicked the cunning brute with his fingers lest the animal should still be alive. Satisfied that it was dead he gently pulled the creature from my ankle like a boy removing a fishhook from a freshly caught carp. He approached me again and held the centipede's lifeless body so that I could examine the insect's sharp incisors – they were like curved needles maybe half an inch in length. On my ankle I could see the evidence of their demonic artistry – two sizeable incisions and an ever-swelling mound.

Tossing the dead centipede over the side of the boat the young man knelt over my ankle, bit down hard on the wound and sucked hard for ten, possibly fifteen seconds. When this was done, he spat out the extracted venom, reached behind him for a bucket of salt, grasped a liberal amount into his hand, rubbed the healing crystals into the wound before pulling me to up my feet and forcing me to hop up and down the deck. After a few moments I was amazed to discover that the numbness in my afflicted limb abated. I resolved to articulate my gratitude and joy to these gentlemen by stepping forward and embracing them one by one. At first they appeared to be a little startled by the gesture, but they soon understood its significance and reciprocated, slapping my back and punching my shoulder. I was naturally of the opinion that my young rescuer was deserving of a more tangible declaration of my indebtedness but I was also cognizant of the uncomfortable fact that what was left of the possessions I'd singled out for inclusion for my hasty departure from Singapore were now lost forever on Lai Ming's raft. I therefore reached into my pocket and gifted the young man with the most valuable item I possessed. My salt-encrusted edition of the Holy Bible.

8. Distant Land.

IDRIFTED IN and out of sleep, wakened only by the occasional crack of a sail and the voices of the men as they traded in the peculiar, and yet beautiful, sounds of their mysterious language. Once, whilst emerging from the realms of sleep, I spied my young rescuer parting the curtains to my cabin and peering in curiously to check my condition. I observed him through half-closed eyes as he entered the cabin with the agility of a cat. He crouched and reached out to feel the material of my waistcoat from Meyer & Mortimer of Conduit Street. He clicked his nails against one of the buttons before leaning in and testing the strength of this curious object with his teeth. Then, startled by a call from one of his companions outside, he sat up and scampered out as silently as he'd entered.

The days crept by as I lay on my makeshift bed of rolled-up netting. By now, thanks to the young fisherman, the episodic spasms of agony in my infected ankle had subsided considerably and I continued to drift in and out of sleep, dreaming occasionally of England, at other times piqued by thoughts of the nefarious treachery of Mr Eustace Skate.

One morning I woke to the smell of fishy broth and, on opening my eyes, I saw a wooden spoon being placed to my lips. Two of the fishermen pulled me up into a sitting posture whilst my rescuer attempted to feed me. I drank as much of the soup as I could. The fishermen spoke gently as I fell back once more into the arms of Morpheus aided by the rocking of the sea and the musical lapping of the water against the sides of the craft.

After what seemed to be many days I was again nudged from my slumbers by the fishermen. I was pulled to my feet and led onto the deck of the small craft. The boat bobbled playfully. The sails clapped out a celebratory rhythm as the circling gulls cackled and screeched. My young rescuer and his companions grinned and directed my gaze towards something in the distance. Shielding my eyes from the glare of the sun I beheld a row of green palm tree shaking their heads in a wild and silent dance on a strip of sandy shore.

9. A letter to my ailing father at Havemore Hall, near Salisbury, Wiltshire.

*D*EAR FATHER– BY now, you have probably received news of the most unfortunate decampment of Mr Eustace Skate from our joint commission. You may also have noticed my failure to note the date of this communication and to present you with even the vaguest indication as to the location of its composition. The unfortunate truth, Sir, is that I am, indeed, presently uncertain of these details myself. I can at least reveal to you that I am on an island and that it has one principal settlement which – as far as I have been able to glean – is named Okeath. It is a sparse collection of huts constructed from wooden frames and insulated with various types of leaves. I estimate vaguely that I have now been in my hut overlooking the port of Okeath for a full month or so and, in that period, there has never been a period of inactivity in the little harbour. Even in the middle of the night I have been torn from my slumbers by the snapped command of a skipper. The fruits of this remarkable assiduity is evident in the barrows of the daily market where all manner of fish are displayed; giant amberjacks and roosterfish, sailfish, snappers, yellow-finned albacores and snooks – their eyes bright as jewels and many of them so fresh as to be still protesting in their baskets!

Each morning – having naturally satiated their own hunger and that of their families – the fishermen, all of them muscular as warriors and possessed of lustrous silver locks, spread out the fruits of their dawn catch and then, by means of a loudly trumpeted conch, the populace of Okeath are summoned to breakfast and soon the beach is thick with smoke bearing the intoxicating aroma of freshly fried fish! A simple life perhaps, but seemingly complete and free from any form of distress.

Following the ritual of breakfast the fishermen's attention is directed towards the filling of an enormous earthenware pot which lies on the sand beneath a neat construction of sticks and branches. Each morning this hungry pot is fed with all manner of vegetables and bones. I can only surmise that a great feast is approaching. Certainly the citizens of Okeath appear to be excited. I am touched by the fact that they are eager to include me, a stranger and outsider, in these mysterious celebrations too. The women and children especially all laugh as they throw their various produce into the pot and, as they do so, they smile in my direction and, naturally, I wave and smile back.

The climate of the island is temperate and warm but once, a few weeks ago, I did observe an alarming phenomenon whereupon the entire archipelago appeared to be in the grip of a tropical gale. This force tore the roofs of some of the huts and snapped the palm trees as if they were nothing but matchsticks! The waves reached terrifying heights and crashed mightily onto the shore. I have deduced from the villagers' paintings and drawings that violent storms are frequent visitors to the island.

My body is slowly recovering from the various punishments it endured at the hands of the ocean and I am hopeful that, soon, my period of convalescence will be at an end. I have increased in bulk as a direct result of the charity of my hosts. They take great interest in my health and well-being and scarcely a day goes by without one of the fishermen prodding my belly to check against any form of malnutrition. The looks of approval these fellows exchange amongst themselves would suggest that I am on the mend and, as soon as I am able, I plan to explore the island further.

In addition to a new pair of trousers – which, miraculously, fit me perfectly – the islanders have kindly supplied me with some of their ink which, I am told, is extracted from a peculiar breed of local octopus but my pot is almost dry and the paper pressed from palm bark is apparently very precious and scare so forgive me if I am forced to draw my letter to a close here. I will roll it carefully into an old porcelain bottle that I found washed up on the shore in a remarkably well-preserved state (complete with stopper) and gently lay it on the waves this afternoon in the hope that it eventually finds its way to English soil. One can only pray that this will be so.

Your humble son,

Hilary.

10. In which a tempting feast is sacrificed for a greater calling.

M Y APPEARANCE IN the harbour early the following morning provoked the usual excitement among the children of Okeath. All silver-haired like their parents, their bare feet slapped the wet sand as they ran towards me and hugged me like a long-lost father betraying none of the diffidence which would have constrained their English counterparts. Of course it was understandable that a mysterious visitor such as myself should inspire such spontaneous explosions of exuberance and I was happy, as ever, to be conducted over to inspect the cavernous earthenware pot and to politely respond to their laughter and incessant pointing. They indicated that I should inspect the interior of the giant pot. Their laughter would then explode once more and I joined in, even popping my head over the brim to look down into the darkness. There appeared to be some form of liquid at the bottom but it was too dark to be certain. The children began to make eating motions, ripping imaginary pieces of flesh apart with their hands, stuffing their mouths and finally rubbing their bellies as if satiated beyond measure. Judging by their hysteria this was a most amusing entertainment and I indulged it to the best of my ability by smiling and contributing the odd chuckle. But truth to tell, I soon grew weary of the game and I wandered down to the sea's edge for a moment of quiet reflection. This was not to be for the exuberant throng of young ruffians followed me. They jumped up and began tugging at my dark hair – a clear novelty on the island – and having amassed sizeable bundles of it they held them aloft like trophies, dancing and whooping! Thankfully ten or so of the fishermen witnessed my plight and raced across the shingle to my rescue. They pulled the frenzied children away and admonished them sternly. Chastised, the impetuous imps were instantly transformed into innocent angels and they hung their heads as they were ordered – one by one – to utter quiet, but nonetheless fearful, apologies. I made light of the affair even though my scalp was still stinging and the young miscreants made their remorseful exit, the stragglers hastened by the perceived threat of a well-aimed foot by one or two of the fishermen.

Once the children were gone the fishermen all appeared to be eager to establish that I had not suffered any lasting physical injury. Their assiduous hands patted my clothes clean of sand and shingle and their fingers prodded my chest and sides and legs. Finally they signalled to each other that they were satisfied with my condition and they all smiled. My young rescuer stepped forward, took my arm and led me eagerly in the direction of a large pan which was sizzling with freshly filleted mackerel pike. He attempted to force me down to a sitting position but I resisted his invitation and attempted to communicate that my intention that day was to embark upon a full and thorough exploration of the island. I pointed firstly at the tall trees on the main body of the island and at the lush abundance of the forest. It appeared that they understood precisely what my ambition was and it was equally apparent that my scheme did not meet their approval. I glanced at each of their displeased faces in turn – particularly at that of my young rescuer – and noted that their earlier aspects of cordiality had been transformed to overwhelming umbrage.

"What is it dear friends?" I implored, although aware that I was incapable of being understood. "How have I offended you? Tell me and I shall gladly apologize!"

Some of the children returned cautiously, no doubt attracted by the aroma of frying fish, and sat down at the edge of our circle, digging up crustaceans from the sand with sticks.

"Gentlemen," I ventured, addressing my audience as if they were a jury at the Old Bailey. "I am naturally very grateful to you for your most remarkable generosity. However, I must nevertheless communicate to you also that it is my avowed duty as an English gentleman to fulfil the conditions of my contract with Julius Colebridge & Sons of Piccadilly and this fulfilment necessitates a thorough exploration of these islands. Rest assured that I intend to carry out the particulars of my chosen course with care, respect and with the utmost consideration for your land, creatures and customs. Now I intend to embark upon this journey of exploration without further ado and, once I have mapped the basic shape and contours of the island, I shall return to you this evening in the fervent hope that my decision to forego this morning feast of your finest mackerel will have been forgiven. Gentlemen, I thank you."

Bowing graciously I turned on my heels and walked away in the direction of the forest. I proceeded with as much dignity as I could muster. I continued to do so even after the dead crab had struck me forcefully on the back of the head.

11. I am steeled by the recollection of Sir Duncan Roseberry's wise words.

A S I ASCENDED the narrow path into the jungle I attempted to resist the conclusion that the accursed plants were somehow deliberately seeking to impede my progress. The sweat lubricated my forehead and it was soon apparent that my poor carcass was unprepared for such an ordeal but I persisted in my task. Why? Firstly, I deduced that an ignominious return to the harbour in such a ragged and defeated manner would have diminished my standing amongst the fishermen. Secondly, I was spurred by my recollection of a distant evening in London when I had witnessed the very final public appearance of Sir Duncan Roseberry before he undertook his fateful journey to the East. His spirit – if indeed he was dead as most of London assumed – was surely looking down upon me at that moment and urging me to take the hard road which led to mystery and, ultimately, to discovery and everlasting fame and glory. That evening in London seemed as distant in time as it did in any measurable form of geography but it was as alive in my imagination as if it had happened the night before.

On that balmy July evening the capital had boasted a most uncommon radiance as I loped over Primrose Hill. Stopping to catch my breath, a cursory glance to my left presented me with a view of the spires of the City of Westminster and it had convinced me that they possessed the same grandeur as anything Venice had to offer. I bounded across the grass, newly liberated from the academic manacles of Cambridge and with the world before me like a nourishing berry ripe for the biting.

Soon I had cobbles under my feet and I joined the throng outside the marble doorway of Haberdasher Hall. Above the archway there hung a large banner bearing the words –

'Tonight – A Public Lecture by the Distinguished traveller and explorer Sir Duncan Roseberry recounting his Incredible Adventures in the Wild jungles of India'.

Many around me said it was the longest banner they could remember. Indeed, I overheard one gentleman me say to his companion that it had taken craftsmen from Dulwich a total of five days to stitch it all into one piece.

Once inside the hall it was immediately evident from the worried demeanour of the proprietor that, in his greed for profit, he had over-filled the venue. We were packed in like sheep and my chest was so tight I hardly had room to breathe! I espied silk-hatted gentlemen and fragrant ladies alongside tradesmen, craftsmen, scribbling journalists and sketch-artists. Only after the heavy oak doors had been closed and securely locked by the perspiring attendants did the unmistakeable figure of Sir Duncan Roseberry stride onto the stage to thunderous applause and whistles from the crowd. Acknowledging them, he slowly unbuttoned his cloak and hung it on a coat-stand behind the lectern. At his partial disrobement several well-born ladies gasped as they glimpsed the merest suggestion of his feted muscularity and their enthusiasm was far from being quelled when Sir Duncan Roseberry pulled back his long golden mane and tied it back in preparation for the delivery of his lecture. Even the mysterious birthmark in the form of an Arabian scimitar which lay across his forehead could not tarnish the great man's physical splendour. If anything, it merely added to it.

And then, of course, he spoke. His voice resonated like the tones of an evenly bowed cello as he recounted his recent journey to the densely vegetated peninsula of Rongathnadoor. At one point, when he stepped forward to the lip of the stage and dropped his voice to a near-whisper to recount the details of his terrifying encounter with the man-eating tiger of Karahimor, one lady by my side swooned and was only revived following the swift application of smelling salts by her companion!

For all the great man's rhetorical skills however, it was his closing paragraph which struck me. Not since Old Jacob's words to me as a child regarding the globe above the stables back at Havemore had I heard such an effective crystallization of the purpose and importance of exploration and discovery.

"Ladies and Gentlemen," he had said. "I am often asked what propels me in my desire to seek out the unknown, the uncharted, the strange and the remote and my answer is always simple. I glory in the act of *discovery*, friends. When I suck the delectable air of danger and adventure into my lungs it is the source of all my energy. Like steam is to the engine, fear and trepidation excites my very soul and propels me to the heart of all that is unfamiliar and rare."

Thunderous applause once again reverberated around Haberdashers Hall and Sir Duncan Roseberry reclaimed his cloak, swung it over his shoulder and exited with a flourish and a bow. Unbeknownst to both himself and his audience of course, it would be his final public engagement before his mysterious expedition to the South Pacific and his subsequent disappearance.

12. I am pursued and attacked by a wild and deadly monster.

IPERCHED SOMEWHAT gingerly upon a fallen palm trunk and took an opportunity to mop my brow. The forest enveloped me and was alive with all manner of alien sounds. Invisible macaws squawked raucously from the heights but my efforts to detect them were entirely in vain for the verdant cupola above me was as high as Filippo Brunelleschi's celebrated dome at the Basilica di Santa Maria del Fiore and splintered with blinding sunlight. Scuttling beetles and cockroaches made their way across the decaying leaves around my feet like devout monks apparently unconcerned by the threat posed by the brown spiders which were coiled like springs in their ghostly webs. I dabbed my forehead and stuffed the sweat-sodden kerchief back in my pocket. The wind teased the tops of the trees, bending them back and then releasing them with malevolent glee of a school bully. Occasionally dislodged fragments of branches, bark and leaves rattled down from the heights like queer hail. In the distance the invisible ocean maintained its unshakeable grip on the island, crashing against the cliffs relentlessly as if its sole intention was reducing the land to rubble and smothering it with its impenetrable depths.

Mopping my brow once more, I continued my explorations for what I calculated to be the best part of an hour before chancing upon the delightful discovery of a small, turbulent stream. Cupping the icy water in my hands I drank greedily and reassured myself that I must have made significant inroads inland because the constant drum of the ocean had diminished and had been overwhelmed by the playful musicality of the tumbling rivulet.

But I was suddenly disturbed by a new sound immediately behind me. Something was approaching through the undergrowth. My over-wrought imagination tormented me by conjuring an image of a tiger or a lion thundering out of the bushes and leaping upon my helpless flesh, ripping it into pieces with sabre-like claws! As the invisible creature approached I scouted around for a weapon – a sharp stick, perhaps, or a rock – but, realizing that there was nothing around I resorted instead to an even more primeval instinct. In short, I *ran*.

I bounded over thicket and bough with surprising agility, encroaching ever deeper into the jungle to escape the invisible monster which was now in full pursuit. Flocks of colourful parrots and kelchacs flapped and screeched in my wake before shooting up into the heights of the trees like fireworks. But my strength quickly dissipated and soon the air became too thin to breathe. I stopped and resigned myself to the knowledge that, despite my apprehensions, I would now be forced to stand my ground and so, as the creature raced towards me through the undergrowth – its rapid approach betrayed by the ominous parting of the vegetation. I stretched up to my full height, tightened both my fists and adopted a rough approximation of the stance I recalled being exemplified by bragging pugilists at Windsor Fair.

Then, like a cannonball out of the darkness the monster was upon me in an instant. He knocked me to the ground.

His claws ripping greedily at my throat.

13. A fierce and dishonourable battle is interrupted by a most edifying sound.

ANY SPECTATOR WHO happened to peek through the undergrowth at that instant would surely have been greatly surprised at the unprepossessing spectacle of a man grappling with a wild porcupine and the indecorous conflict swiftly descended into a series of scratches, blows and bites. Finally, we both became enmeshed in a clench which caused us to roll down a slope into the waters of a stagnant pool. I gulped for air and tried in vain to establish any kind of equilibrium as my feet slid along the mud. But then, just as I imagined that my strength was failing and that I should end my days as a cluster of bones on a desolate and uncharted island, I heard a most welcoming sound. For the first time since my arrival on the island I heard the wondrous melody of the English language and my heart swelled. Surely, I concluded, civilization could not be far away if the Queen's English was spoken – even if, in this instance, if it was filtered through the brash tones of an American accent.

"Hold your damn thrashing sir or I shall never spike this devil!"

I obeyed his command despite the discomfort of being gnawed by a wild and determined beast. As the porcupine pressed his teeth into my throat with refreshed vehemence I heard the brash American tones ring out again –

"Die, you prickly varmint!"

The porcupine stiffened briefly, releasing a plaintive and somewhat heart-breaking cry of pain and surprise before breathing his last. My American saviour gripped his spines, tore him from my body and dropped him into the pool a few feet away as if he was nothing but a stuffed plaything from the nursery.

"Why, thank you sir."

"Don't mention it. Come on, take my hand. They got poisonous lizards in them ponds that don't take kindly to being disturbed."

I allowed myself to be winched out of the muddy pond and, for the first time, I was able to fully observe my rescuer.

He was wearing a rather tattered naval uniform and appeared to possess that sinewy strength so common to maritime men. Tearing off a leaf from one of the bushes he wiped the porcupine's blood from his sabre before sliding it back into the scabbard on his belt.

"Hell," he said, spitting a stream of brown tobacco onto the grass. "You sure got on the wrong side of Maximillian the Second."

"Maximillian the Second? I'm afraid you have me at something of a disadvantage."

"I am referring," said the American, "to that poor critter who now lies floatin' in this pool. A most faithful fellow he was too. May the Lord have mercy on his soul – if the Good Lord decreed that such lowly individuals were worthy of souls of course. I believe the matter is the subject of passionate debate these days."

"You... *knew* this porcupine?"

"You bet I did," said the American, thumping his sodden boots on the bank. "And, until this ill-advised display of aggression, a very fine and valued associate he was too. I named him Maximillian the Second in honour of the previous curator of that sobriquet, another noble porcupine which was sadly crushed by a palm tree shortly after my arrival on these godforsaken shores. But I see I am ahead of myself."

He extended his hand, spat out another stream of tobacco and grinned expansively to display a row of brown and uneven teeth.

"Samuel Burgess of the United States Navy, pleased to make your acquaintance."

"Durwood," I replied, still moderately overawed by the bizarre procession of the day's events, "Hilary Durwood."

"Well Mr Durwood," said Mr Burgess, "help me get poor Maximillian the Second out of this pool. Then perhaps you may care to join me for supper."

14. I am offered a rare opportunity to expound my philosophical views.

"I CAN SEE that Maximillian the Second is providing you with some difficulty Mr Durwood," said Mr Burgess, smiling as the juice ran down his chin and bib and sizzled in the flames which now crackled between us on the beach. "But then in truth I guess he always was a tough little devil. The obstinacy of his flesh is probably on account of all the rats he consumed."

"*Rats?*"

"Why yes," said the American, slicing off another sinewy strip of flesh from the spitted carcass of the porcupine by means of his dagger and chewing it with no apparent sense of unease. "Maximillian the Second, like his predecessor, was the scourge of all the rodents in this patch. Herbivore by nature, he nevertheless developed something of a liking for their flesh. Why, I do recall that one memorable night he caught and devoured no less than five!"

He raised his glass to the evening sky.

"Maximillian the Second – we pay our respects to you sir!"

I followed suit and toasted the beast with a rather excellent 1836 Chateau Canet Minervois. Mysteriously, Mr Burgess appeared to possess limitless quantities of that most excellent vintage and, following our enthusiastic consumption of two full bottles, my mind was somewhat addled. My sense of vision had also deteriorated and, as we feasted on the beach, the black waves of the Pacific crashed relentlessly like frothing cavalry intent on our destruction.

Mr Burgess signaled the end of his supper with a confident belch as loud as ripped canvas. Wiping his mouth on his bib he sat back, reached into his pocket, retrieved a slim cheroot, and lit it.

"Mr Durwood," he said, after a thoughtful interval. "You strike me as an educated fellow. What, would you propose, is the driving force of a man's ambition?"

"You flatter me sir," I said.

In truth I was glad of the opportunity to put down my plate and draw a veil over what had been, conceivably, one of the most repulsive and indigestible dishes it had ever been my misfortune to endure. I cleared my throat.

"If I had to venture an opinion on this matter Mr Burgess, as indeed you have invited me to do so, I would agree with the oft-expressed convictions of wiser minds that ambition may be spurred by many causes – chief amongst them the desire for wealth, power and influence. But in my own case the ambition of pursuing a literary career is not motivated by any of these factors but is, rather, fuelled by that most futile of human fancies – the craving for immortality. A vain and futile ambition it must be conceded but surely, during his brief tenure in this world, a man may make a mark Mr Burgess? A line in the sand like the one I produce now with this stick. Inevitably, this mark will be a little fainter tomorrow – and, who knows, it may well have disappeared entirely by the middle of next week – but I can at the very least take some satisfaction in the fact that it was there after I had moved on and I can only wish that whatever work I may produce may similarly survive my earthly form and inspire other men in the future."

After a short pause, Mr Burgess responded with laughter. He slapped his knee in the raucous manner of a seaman.

"Mr Durwood', he exclaimed, "I can see that I was correct to judge you as a most capable philosopher! I am heartened by this confirmation, and I am consoled also by the very fact that we have one important thing in common."

"We do?"

"Indeed. Come Mr Durwood. I have something which may well be of interest to you."

15. I make the acquaintance of a most remarkable lady.

IFOLLOWED THE American up the beach towards a slim entrance to a cave which was illuminated by two ship's lanterns.

"I apologize for the unrefined nature of my quarters but, like yourself Mr Durwood, I am a victim of circumstance."

"On the contrary. I would conclude that you had succeeded in creating a most delightful abode."

Mr Burgess was clearly a gentleman of great fortitude and industry for, out of such an unpromising foundation as a mere crack in the ancient rock of the island's shoreline he had created a dwelling which – were it not for the noticeable absence of windows – would not have been incongruent in some of the smartest crescents of Mayfair. The floors were richly carpeted in an assortment of silken rugs which I imagined having been fashioned in the bazaars of Constantinople or the markets of Marrakech. An elaborate and exquisite silver chandelier hung down from the roof of the cave like a peculiarly crafted stalactite and the flames of its candles were undisturbed by the gales which had risen out of nowhere and which now raged and whistled outside. The walls were festooned with drawings and paintings of all sizes on paper and canvas and towering above all the other exhibits was a large wooden sculpture of a lady painted in blue, flesh, and gold – her robes stretching back like folded wings as she prepared to swoop down from the heights.

"Ah," said the American, having followed my gaze and reaching up to pat the gracious lady rather indelicately with his hand until she rocked on her supporting ropes. "I see that you Mr Durwood, like all other men who come into contact with her, have fallen in love with the delectable Lady Mathilda – esteemed mast-head on the fine vessel *Great Plains*!"

"She is most striking."

"That she undoubtedly is, Mr Durwood. And all the crew, from Captain Morwelly down to the powder monkeys, invested her with great wisdom as well as beauty. We sailors are men of great superstition, and we believe that, if we pray and follow the rules of the sea, we will be guided eventually across its hazards to the green hills of home. Alas, this poor lady was too trusting of the wicked servants of fate and, through no fault of her own – thanks to the forceful Pacific gales – we discovered ourselves stranded in shallow waters. But Lady Mathilda did not dishonour herself for her intentions were pure and she redeemed herself by leading us to within half a mile of this island – a barren and devilish plot of land I grant you – but land nonetheless."

"How did you retrieve her?"

The American laughed and slapped me heartily – rather too heartily it must be declared – on the shoulder.

"With extreme difficulty Mr Durwood! That's your answer! With *extreme difficulty*!"

He laughed again and it swiftly degenerated into a cough.

"I swam out to the stricken vessel through the treacherous currents of the bay and recovered her by means of a saw and some ropes. Then, just as the tides advanced, I lowered her into one of the rowboats and brought her back to shore."

'An impressive deed Mr Burgess."

"Perhaps you wouldn't comprehend but, to a sailing man like myself, the Lady Mathilda was tantamount to representing the spirit of our ship and, to the sailor, the ship represents his very soul. As I observed the *Great Plains* languishing before my eyes, day after day and night after night in this cursed bay, it pained me to watch Lady Mathilda sinking ever further into the water. She was the first item I retrieved although, as you may see, since then she has been augmented by one or two accessories."

He cackled again and laid a hand on my shoulder.

"But I did not lure you into my cavern to dazzle your eyes with the good Lady Mathilda. No sir, I desire to share with you the true treasures of this craggy hole."

He pulled back a heavy curtain of ship sail and ushered me quickly into the inner sanctum of his hermitage.

16. The mockery of love.

A S I PROGRESSED into the cavernous sanctuary, I perceived an enormous pot suspended over some charred logs, like the one I had seen on the beach in the village. Alongside it there was a long table adorned with a neat array of knives next to a big black book.

Gazing up at the walls I saw that, from the floor up to a height of approximately nine feet, there was not a single bare stretch of stone to be seen. Both sides of the cavern were layered with a ghoulish chainmail of interlocking skeletons of all sizes suspended from thick trunks of wood. There were birds ranging from wren-sized creatures through to gigantic albatrosses and tall ostriches together with several other more mysterious species. There were also the mortal frames of mammals, both land-bound and marine. I identified voles, water rats, seals, porpoises, wild bores, monkeys, bottlenose dolphins and – most spectacular of all (suspended from a giant hook, its head but a few inches away from the ground) – the impressive carcass of a baby humpback whale. As I cautiously made my way along this macabre exhibition towards the far side of the chamber, I noticed that there were hundreds upon hundreds of fish too; warbonnets, gunnels, sandabbs, lingcods and stingrays together with bonitos, barracudas, and sharks. I stopped beside the pot and peered inside, and my anxiety was immediately translated into revulsion for there – entwined at the bottom in a sickening parody of amity – lay the crumpled remains of two human beings, both still wearing the ragged remains of their uniforms. Suddenly there was a hand on my shoulder. I recoiled like an affrighted child.

"Well?" asked the American, his face flickering eerily in the half-shadows incited by the candles. "What are your impressions?"

I attempted rather vainly to appear as unconcerned as possible, but I was naturally disturbed by the presence of the two unfortunate souls whose bones now lay at the bottom of the pot.

"Sir," he said, with a slow smile, "I have recognized in you a kindred spirit."

"You have?"

"We are both driven by our passions. In your case it is a literary and exploratory intuition and mine are of a slightly different nature, although no less intense. Allow me a moment to elucidate."

17. *Being the full extent of Mr Samuel Burgess's elucidation.*

"I WAS BORN on a farm, Mr Durwood, and raised the hard way in Forsyth County, North Carolina. My father was a fine, but robust, individual with an affinity towards the land, rearing cattle and growing his tobacco and sweet potatoes so that I and my five brothers could have a respectable and comfortable home after my poor mother – God rest her soul – relinquished her hold on this mortal burden. My poor Daddy was poorly educated but I can proclaim that he was endowed with the unadorned wit of one whose rhetoric had not been honed by scholars but, rather, by the wind which forced its way across the land from the plains of South Dakota and by the crystal waters of the river which cascaded off the Blue Ridge Mountains. His abiding hope was that I, as his eldest son, would one day inherit the farm and continue to till the land but fate intervened.

One afternoon I accompanied my Daddy and some of his workmen to the nearest town of Hampsville on our buck-wagon. Now to call Hampsville a *town* would be to invest the place with too much importance since, in truth, it was a mere few streets comprising some hardware stores, a jail, a saloon and – I am ashamed to confess, Sir – a cathouse of the most disreputable manner. But, that afternoon, the black hand of fate ensured that my gaze was diverted towards a spectacle outside the saloon which, once witnessed, ensured that I would leave the farm and North Carolina forever. You see, sir, that day, the town of Hampsville played host to a travelling Medicine Show. The tumblers and conjurers were very remarkable fellows but, memorable and diverting as they were, they were as nothing compared to the oriental gentleman who then stepped forward as part of the show and proclaimed, in his excellent English, that he had come all the way from China with the sole intention of demonstrating the culinary treasures of his homeland. My diet was a simple one based around the sweet potato, chicken, pork and beef but this gentleman – who informed us that his name was Fu Kwek – changed everything. Since then, I have travelled the world and sampled the cuisines of various lands, but I believe we never forget our moment of induction into a new and heavenly domain and, that day, as my tongue teased out all possible variations of flavour from those mesmerizing spices which Fu Kwek conjured up, my life was transformed. I forgot everything about tilling the land. My curiosity had been aroused Mr Durwood and I had developed a desire to investigate all possible flavours of the known world!

"The very next night I snuck out of my bed when everyone in the house was asleep. I packed some nuts and fruit from the larder into a kerchief sack, secured a pair of spare boots and pants and stepped out into the night, eager not to stir the raucous alarum of the cockerel. I saddled up Hank – the swiftest horse in the stable – mounted him and spurred him on through the gates, along the track, through the dead streets of Hampsville and on towards the plain until, at dawn, we finally reached the Port of Wilmington. There, by the banks of Cape Fear River, I joined the US Navy as an Apprentice Third Class. They were eager for recruits at the time Mr Durwood and didn't ask any awkward questions on account of the need to quell the threat posed to American trade by fearless buccaneers on the South China Seas.

I was immediately put to work scrubbing the deck but having been informed of my culinary ambitions, Captain Morwelly of the *Great Plains* looked kindly upon me and placed me under the guardianship of the cook Mr Jubal Slerk.

"I learned to cook under Mr Jubal Slerk's expert tuition. Prior to his naval career Mr Slerk had been a chef at a reputable hotel in New Orleans and mealtimes on board the *Great Plains* became a wonder to behold as the men formed eager lines stretching from the central masthead right back to the stern – all of them clutching their bowls and speculating as to what gastronomic miracle Mr Slerk had once again created. Whenever we stopped at various islands and ports along the way in our pursuit of the merciless pirates, Mr Slerk always took advantage of the opportunity to venture inland to secure an abundance of fruit or vegetables which, with my assistance, he then carried on board the *Great Plains* and kept fresh in his larder with the aid of some scattered ice. It is fair to say that the US Navy is many things to many men. For some it may represent an escape whilst for others it can be a living Hell. For me, it was my education. The *Great Plains* my Harvard and Yale and Mr Jubal Slerk was my professor. Under his tutelage I became a skilful culinarian in my own right and, after three years of our lonely mission in the south Pacific I had already commenced my life's mission to catalogue each fruit, meat and vegetable known to mankind. At the end of each day I would record by candlelight my impressions of new flavours and textures. This volume began as a mere few pages but then, over weeks and months and years, it became sizeable enough to necessitate the leather binding you see before you here in this black book. Naturally, it is an impossible task to fulfil but there are always new tastes and textures to be discovered just as for you there are new mountains, valleys, oceans and islands to be sighted, mapped and chronicled. This book will be my particular 'line in the sand' Mr Durwood and it won't surprise you to learn that, since my arrival on this island, I have continued my work and what you see arrayed on these walls are the remains of all the curious new beasts I have added to my epicurean thesaurus.

"Ah, but I see that you are weary after the night's adventures and that I am but a troublesome obstacle between you and the restful arms of Hypnos! Follow me and you will notice that I have attached a large hammock here between these two posts. I am aware that you are not a seafaring gentleman Mr Durwood but let me reassure you that it is a most comfortable berth once your form has grown accustomed to its peculiar constitution."

18. My struggles with a hammock precede a most alarming hallucination and a rude awakening.

I QUICKLY CONCLUDED that attempting to predict and negotiate the ebb and flow of a hammock was beyond the capabilities of logic or science. Within a matter of seconds my exhausted bulk lay trapped like a helpless pea in its enveloping pod and the dastardly cot appeared to be mocking my efforts at securing any form of comfort. But, bothersome as the insolent hammock was, it would be wrong to place the entire burden of blame for my insomnia on its shoulders for, in truth, the eerie collection of bones which were suspended from the walls of the chamber also played a part. By the flickering illuminations of the candles suspended from the roof of the chamber in their incongruous chandeliers I saw the grimacing death masks of all the fearsome menagerie – some in half-shadow, others in silhouette – and my alarmed imagination fancied that perhaps they were not dead at all! I imagined that the outstretched wings of the seabirds began to flutter. They swooped down with their hook-like talons and savage beaks poised to tear into my soft flesh! The bones of the elongated serpents disengaged themselves from their hooks and slithered down towards me, entwining around my throat, tightening their grip until both my eyes were plucked from their sockets like obscene fruit! I threw my bulk from side to side in an effort to liberate myself but, tragically, my determination proved to be my undoing for I capsized and sank to the ground with surprising swiftness precipitating a loud and somewhat sickening crack from my skull.

"Mr Durwood! Mr Durwood!"

I opened my eyes and discovered Mr Burgess leaning over me, his breath pungent with tobacco.

"Wake up! There's danger! They're here!"

His urgency was quelled momentarily by the sight of my forehead.

"Why Mr Durwood," said Mr Burgess, "you are wounded."

I investigated the source of my discomfort with the tips of my fingers and discovered a paste of blood in my hair.

"I have to report Sir', I said, somewhat drowsily, "that my encounter with the hammock was not a happy one."

I imagined that a slight smile had encroached the otherwise grim demeanour of the American but I swiftly concluded that this was no time for rancour and, within seconds, Mr Burgess had helped me to my feet and had thrusted a bayonetted musket into my hands.

"Are you a hunting man Mr Durwood?"

"Not especially."

"Then it is a happy coincidence that your musket is not loaded. But they won't know that. Come, follow me."

My confused expression prompted a swift explanation as we moved towards the mouth of the cave and out onto the dark, windswept beach.

"Where are we going?" I asked, desperately trying to keep pace with the American. "Are we on the trail of vicious beasts?"

"The most vicious of them all," said Mr Burgess. "We are on the trail of men."

19. My first murder.

"COME SIR," said the American. "They are very close now. Hold tight to that musket and keep your bayonet poised."

The trees hissed like cobras and the lower branches clacked their sabres.

"They are in these woods," said Mr Burgess, halting me with his arm. "And by God's good grace I shall flush the devils out! Wait here Mr Durwood. Keep that bayonet primed and listen for my command. Above all else, remember that whatever occurs here tonight, you must stand your ground – do you understand me sir? *Stand your ground!*"

Before I'd had a chance to protest Mr Burgess was swallowed by the dark jungle.

"Come you silver-haired devils! Taste the bitter tang of steel!"

His voice boomed out of the darkness and it was followed by the deadly crack of his musket. Invisible nocturnal birds cawed in alarm from the heights and crashed chaotically into the branches causing a shower of feathers and leaves which cascaded down over my head and arms. Then, gradually, they ceased their panic and the chirruping insects could be heard again above the constant rumble of the ocean and the wheezing of my chest. For a few seconds I was too afraid to move but then I was drawn deeper into the jungle by the distinctive smell of gunpowder.

"Is it done?" I whispered, standing next to Mr Burgess.

"Ran like kids," he said. "Except for one. The ringleader I guess. Wily as a Comanche."

He gripped my arm.

"Hear that?"

"What?"

Then I heard a shuffling in the undergrowth about ten or fifteen yards away.

"He's gonna come at us! He's like a cornered catamount! Raise that bayonet Mr Durwood and, by God, make it count or, surely, we will both be done for!"

Instinctively I thrusted my bayonet forward in a series of somewhat clumsy motions. I had expected them to be largely ornamental and wholly subservient to Mr Burgess's more accomplished tactics but then, much to my horror and surprise, I felt the sensation of the bayonet tearing through flesh, ripping into organs and scraping against a stubbornly resistant spine! My victim fell to the ground before me, dragging down the musket with his weight as he groaned and succumbed to stillness.

"Why Mr Durwood," said Mr Burgess, expressing both surprise and satisfaction. "I believe you have killed him."

Unleashing a full-throated cackle he slapped me heartily on the back as if I'd bagged a pheasant. The action prompted a tumultuous reaction in the pit of my stomach and I was forced to bend over and vomit most forcefully.

"You can be proud Mr Durwood."

"*Proud?*" I exclaimed, stretching to my full height again and wiping my mouth with my sleeve. "I must tell you Mr Burgess that I fail sense any pride in this action at all! A man lies *dead*! Are you truly aware of that fact sir?"

"You don't understand."

"I understand well enough the immorality of my actions and the consequences for my mortal soul!"

The American stepped forward and the faint moonlight betrayed his wry smile.

"Your eloquence in this moment of personal crisis does you much credit Mr Durwood. However, I suggest that we venture back to the cave before this unfortunate scoundrel's companions return for vengeance."

He brushed past but I restrained him.

"But surely we cannot simply leave him here?"

Mr Burgess shrugged.

"What do you propose?"

"A Christian burial sir! It's the least we can do!"

The American was disconcerted. Although I also sensed that he was eager to depart the scene quickly without a tiresome debate.

"Very well Mr Durwood," he said, with a resigned sigh. "Take his arms and I shall take the legs."

20. A terrifying discovery.

WEIGHED DOWN BY the melancholy cargo, our progress along the jungle path was slower than we would have wished. The dead man's limbs and sinews were stiffening and his body was as heavy as a sack of coal. Despite this inconvenience however, I remained true to my conviction that the fellow – whatever his beliefs – should receive the dignity of a Christian burial.

We finally emerged from the jungle and stood upon a small cliff overlooking the beach. Out in the bay I noticed that the wooden hulk of the *Great Plains* was being buffeted violently and that the waves had suddenly increased in force. They pummelled the hull with white-tipped fury, tossing the wreck from side to side like a plaything. In the distance there was thunder, rolling like invisible boulders of granite across the skies. The clouds were black.

"This is as good a spot as any I guess Mr Durwood."

We placed the body as gently as we could upon a strip of soil above the sand and, as the curtain of silver hair fell away, I studied his face for the first time in the dim light.

"What is it?" said Mr Burgess, noting my shocked demeanour with no little amusement. "Have you not seen a dead face before? Come, seeing as you insist on a Christian burial, clear away these stones whilst I go down to fetch a shovel."

As the American departed in huge, angry strides I knelt and gazed at the face of the man I had murdered in the vain hope that there had been a mistake. But alas, no. My initial conclusion was confirmed – this indeed was the body of the young fisherman who had saved my life. I had returned his kindness by depriving him of his own. Guilt and remorse now rocked my soul like the mighty waves assaulted the shell of the *Great Plains* out in the bay. The young fisherman gazed up at me with his unseeing eyes – blind not only to the magical beauty of God's creation but also to the majesty of his words contained in the Holy Bible I had given him. The Holy Bible which lay tucked in his blood-soaked belt.

How long did I stand there and gaze – my heart pounding and tears streaming down my cheeks? It is impossible to calculate. Mr Burgess eventually returned with a spade and we took turns in digging.

As I stood beside the finished grave and patted the dirt from my hands I concluded that, due to the force of the gales which were now lashing us from the open ocean, there was every likelihood that the modest shrine with its simple wooden cross would soon be blown away and eradicated from all human memory. But the same gales which could level temples and cities and all manner of mankind's vanities could never eradicate my shame and sense of unworthiness. God would find a way to punish me for my sin. He would cast my soul to the devil but, before that, I was sure that he would make my earthly existence even more miserable than it had recently become.

The American placed a brotherly arm on my shoulder.

"What you need is some strong coffee. I have some fine Kona from Hawaii in my larder."

I allowed myself to be led down the winding path towards the entrance to the cave, closing my eyes to protect them from the sheets of sharp, glassy sand that were being whipped across my face by the gales. We entered and Mr Burgess lit a fire to boil some water in an earthen pot whilst I listened to the cruel howling of the gales as they taunted the island like wolves.

"Drink sir," said Mr Burgess, placing a steaming cup of black coffee in my hand. "This is elixir is renowned for its recuperative qualities."

"Thank you," I replied, "although I fear that my despair lies far beyond the alleviative powers of any beverage."

"Perhaps so, but I sincerely believe that you acted purely in self-defence tonight and I have no doubt that the good Lord will take it into account on Judgement Day. Besides, I have a tale to tell which might make you re-evaluate your sense of desolation."

"I doubt it sir," I said, sipping the bitter coffee.

"I shall take that as a challenge Mr Durwood. And so I shall begin."

21. In which Mr Samuel Burgess is revealed as a gentleman of great intuition and erudition.

"AS IS THE case with most tales of maritime misadventure Mr Durwood, the circumstances of my arrival upon these shores was more the product of accident rather than deliberation. In short, sir, it was the result of a storm. A most hellish storm the like of which Captain Morwelly and the crew of the *Great Plains* had never experienced! The waves were as high as the Appalachian peaks but, unlike those sedentary giants, these particular mountains were constantly shifting – ever-changing monsters which raged and crashed against the cracking bow and stern of our ship, ripping down the masts and washing away all that was not tied up along the deck. I witnessed many a fine and strong sailor being swept away and had I not had the good sense to tie my arms to the helm I am certain that I too would have been snatched and hurled to the impenetrable depths. The storm raged for three full days and three full nights and during that period I steered the ship as best I could, the ropes which tied me to the helm tearing into my flesh and drawing blood and the salty ocean crashing down upon me from all directions. Poor old Captain Morwelly attempted to come to my aid by running up the companionway from lower deck but he was caught by the vicious storm and I saw him tossed out into the black oblivion – his arms flailing wildly until he vanished forever. The same gruesome inevitability befell Clark, the burly helmsman, and all three of the young ensigns – Barrett, Launceston and Howell. I must have been overwhelmed by exhaustion for the next thing I knew, the *Great Plains* lay nestling in the comparatively sheltered waters of this bay. Naturally, having been ravaged by the open ocean she was much damaged and, truth to tell, it was clear that she was in no condition to persevere with her mission. The whirling tempest had rendered the vessel unseaworthy and now the keel scraped the rocks at the bottom of the bay. The masthead was snapped and the sails lay drooping in the water like dying swans. Upon reassembling on the deck of the ship that morning, it became evident that the superior officer among our depleted crew was Sergeant Smethwick. His first decision was to lower one of the rowing boats and take five marines with him to investigate the alien terrain of the island. Mr Jubal Slerk stood alongside me and we observed Sergeant Smethwick and his men as they rowed across the bay towards shore with their bayonetted muskets held high. When they eventually returned the Sergeant was pleased to report that the island itself featured lush vegetation and delicious fruit but, most fortuitously of all, they had encountered a friendly band of remarkable silver-haired local folk who had lavished upon them such hospitality the likes of which they had never previously encountered."

"The following day another party ventured onto the island under Sergeant Smethwick's command and, this time, Mr Jubal Slerk and I were permitted to be among their number. When greeted by the locals they lavished upon us yet another feast which, I was told, was even more grand than the one they had produced the previous day. Generous hunks of roast wild hog were served with ripe peaches and sweet pears – each one spiced with ginger and pungent peppercorns. I saw mounds of fresh coconut sliced into juicy segments and an orange-like fruit which neither I nor Mr Jubal Slerk had ever before sampled but whose sweetness infused our bodies like purest nectar. But the most remarkable aspect of this curious, but pleasing, gesture was that – far from being merely a singular exhibition of native compliance and consideration from our hosts – it was duly lavished upon us daily with admirable enthusiasm. Every morning the islanders greeted us in their hollowed-out canoes and guided us through the jungle pathways to their village. There, upon the beach and sheltered from the extremities of the sun by the protective palm leaves of the huts, the entire surviving crew of the *Great Plains* were served with spiny lobsters, sleek, pan-fried bonito, butterflied angelfish, swordfish and shark. During the following month or so I observed, with no small sense of trepidation Mr Durwood, that the diminished crew of the *Great Plains* – including Sergeant Smethwick and his small contingent of men – appeared to have been seduced by the potency and regularity of this unexpected welcome because they were now as indolent and dazed as those poor wretches who are in the thrall of devilish opiates. I argued that we should fulfil our duty and proceed to repair the storm-damaged vessel but our pleas fell on deaf ears. Sergeant Smethwick swept aside these protests as if they were no more than the troublesome fire-flies.

"My fervent hope was that Smethwick and his men would eventually weary of their hedonistic pursuits but no, far from tiring of the generosity of the islanders, the increasingly corpulent and lazy bunch were now reliant on these daily feasts. Indeed, some of the men were no longer taking the trouble to return to the ship at night electing instead to sleep in these caves along the beach. This would have disastrous and horrific consequences which no man could ever have foreseen.

"But come Mr Durwood, it has been a long and eventful night and I can see that your eyes are becoming heavy. Perhaps a few hours rest in the hammock may be in order so that you may recuperate and regain your physical and intellectual powers before I conclude my tale tomorrow."

The American led me to the hammock like an executioner to the block.

22. I encounter yet another fearsome monster.

THE OCCASIONAL FLASH of lightning revealed the huge green waves upon which I was tossed around like a cork. Lai Ming had returned and, beside him on the rickety raft, his evil hound barked silently and continuously. Meanwhile, the tumbling clouds hurled even more water down onto the already brimming tub of the Pacific Ocean. I rolled – first to the left, then to the right – before falling...falling...

...and hitting the floor with a thump.

A lighted candle suddenly revealed the flickering face of Mr Burgess. He was in his gown and wearing a nightcap.

"A nightmare Mr Durwood?"

He cackled and laid his candle to one side.

"Hammocks are like horses. You must gain their trust. But once that has been achieved then you will be guaranteed their complete devotion."

The American's wiry strength guided me to my feet but as he patted the dust away from the striped pyjamas he had kindly lent me from the *Great Plains* store I became aware of two glowing jewels in the darkness a mere five or six yards away. From the same source, I heard a low and constant rumble.

"Do not be alarmed," said Mr Burgess, noticing my apprehension and puzzlement, "allow me to introduce you to Mr Delphus of Clare. A most remarkable gentleman."

I beheld the largest cat I had ever seen in my life.

"A *cat* sir?" I said, backing away instinctively. "But surely that is... *a lion?*"

Mr Burgess cackled again.

"Stroke him there. Just here beneath the jaw. That's where he appreciates it the most."

"Are you quite sure?"

"Don't be afraid."

I stepped forward and cautiously did as I had been instructed and the enormous cat rumbled like a volcano. I wasn't sure if it was a purr or a growl. I pulled back my hand like a whip.

"He is certainly a most… *impressive* specimen," I ventured.

As the curious cat approached me I saw that he was suffering with a limp to his back leg. He rubbed his huge head against my hand and encouraged me to stroke him once more. Mr Burgess cackled.

"My intention was to continue my tale in the morning Mr Durwood but, seeing as we have now been joined by Mr Delphus of Clare – a creature who plays no small part in my tale as you will shortly discover – perhaps it may be appropriate and convenient to conclude my humble history right now?"

"By all means."

23. A continuation of Mr Burgess's tale.

"IT WAS A desperate situation Mr Durwood, and Mr Jubal Slerk and I concluded that it required a swift response. Whilst our lethargic shipmates might have been happy, in their absence, to allow the waves to pound the *Great Plains* into smithereens the noble chef and I dived into the surf and swam against the tide in the vain hope that perhaps we may be able to minimize the damage by somehow towing the great ship further into calmer waters. But the more we tried to swim the more the ocean pushed us back and so we decided that a modified plan would have to be implemented. We resolved that the most realistic option was to salvage as much of the cargo as we could and hope that, at a subsequent date, we could return to attempt a reprise of our original plan when the ship was lighter and more manoeuvrable.

"So, for three or four days we repeated our mission. We swam out to the ship and reclaimed items which may be useful such as muskets, hammocks, items of clothing, food and suchlike. The task became less arduous when we gathered up some pieces of wood from the ship's hull and constructed a raft. I was always a practical man Mr Durwood and construction was always one of my skills. The raft was simple but effective and it enabled Mr Slerk and I to retrieve objects which some, I do not wonder, would claim to be somewhat inessential such as my collection of animals which so astounded you on your arrival Mr Durwood."

"And it still does sir, I have to confess."

"And this was how we discovered this fine fellow."

Mr Burgess stroked the chin of the enormous cat again and Mr Delphus of Clare responded by releasing a purr which sounded like the grinding of rocks.

"This resourceful beast had survived by virtue of a regular supply of fresh fish. Judging by his increased size he had clearly enjoyed a healthier diet than the one he had experienced prior to our misfortune. But his temperament had altered too. Whereas before he had been at least relatively docile and tolerant of his human companions on the ship Mr Delphus of Clare was now transformed into a feral and hissing demon! At first neither Mr Slerk nor I could figure it out. However, we succeeded eventually in coaxing him onto the raft and, once ashore, I discovered the root of the cat's new-found acerbity. He had been wounded sir. The same wound that afflicts his back leg now. See how he flinches if I go near it?"

To demonstrate, Mr Burgess went as if to stroke the cat's hind leg but, before he could reach, the wounded animal hissed at him, raising his armed claw, baring his teeth and emitting a threatening roar.

"I can only hope that the poor creature's wound will heal of its own accord Mr Durwood."

"But what of Mr Slerk? Is he still on the island?"

"Indeed he is Mr Durwood. His body at least."

Mr Burgess sighed deeply and shook his head. After a few seconds of reflection he looked up at me and continued.

"It was all on account of some spoons. To the average man like myself they are items for everyday use eliciting no more curiosity or controversy than a humble jug or cup. But to a chef of Mr Jubal Slerk's stature, the implements of his craft were crucial and the silver set of cutlery he had received as a gift from the Spanish court as an expression of their gratitude following a feast Mr Slerk had provided for their representatives in Cadiz were particularly precious to him and he could not bear the thought of them being lost to the sea.

"Mr Slerk had forsaken the raft and had swum out to the *Great Plains* three or four times to retrieve this treasured set and, one by one, he had succeeded in rescuing all the pieces but the fate of the spoons was still unknown. Time and time again I watched him brave the waters for one more attempt to find them. I warned him of the dangers but Mr Slerk was a stubborn man.

"One morning, a full month or so after Sergeant Smethwick's mutinous abscondment, the waters in the bay were unusually calm. Under these circumstances it proved more difficult than usual for me to attempt to persuade Mr Slerk against his tenacious efforts to retrieve his precious spoons. Laughing off my cautionary words he referred me to the tranquility of the waters, peeled off his outer garments and guided his not insignificant bulk into the water. Within a matter of seconds his head was a bobbing ball amid the glinting blue waters. And then, in an instant, he was gone."

Mr Burgess paused for longer than I'd anticipated.

"Gone sir?"

"Sharks," he said. "The tigers of the deep. The following morning the lapping waves retrieved what was left of Mr Slerk's remains and I buried the honourable gentleman. In three separate boxes."

24. *In which my tie and a block of wood prove to be of great benefit.*

NIGHTMARES OF SHARKS, spoons and dismemberment were swiftly curtailed by the tyrannical grip of gravity as, once again, I was turfed from my hammock and hurled to the ground. I was about to get up to my feet when I was surprised by a sudden brush of fur crossing the back of my hand. The sound of grinding rocks informed me that I was sitting next to Mr Delphus of Clare.

"My dear fellow," I said softly, so as not to alarm it unnecessarily, "you gave me quite a fright."

Outside the wind howled like a million lost souls but this sound was now augmented by a moan of anguish from the cat. As my eyes became more accustomed to the dark I noticed the animal limping in a circle as he tried to settle down.

"You poor chap," I said.

I was no surgeon and I had never received any medical instruction but back home at Havemore I had often observed Old Jacob, our stalwart gamekeeper, treating stricken creatures and I recalled how once he came across a wounded deer in Halestock Wood at the southern extremity of my father's land. The beast had been a fine one, a female of maybe a year and a half but she had clearly misjudged her footing whilst attempting to run away at our approach and she now lay prostrate on the leaves. Her brown eye watched helplessly as we crouched down and her legs twitched instinctively but, as they did, the pain became more intense and the animal unleashed a cry of agony. Old Jacob had uttered some words of comfort and placed his hand on the deer's head.

"Will she die Jacob?"

"Perhaps," he said. "Fetch me that stick."

I obeyed and handed it to him.

"Hold on to it a second."

From his pocket he produced a roll of bale string and bit off a piece. Lifting the deer's wounded leg he somehow managed – despite the animal's terrified protestations – to slip one piece of string underneath it. Motioning for me to give him the stick, Old Jacob placed it firmly against the deer's damaged leg and secured it with the bale string. When I next returned home from school at Christmas, Old Jacob beckoned me over one afternoon and led me along the forest path until we saw the same deer contentedly tugging some leaves from the branches above her head and chewing them with obvious delight.

It was approaching dawn but not yet light and so it was almost impossible to discern what lay around me but, as I reached out carefully into various boxes and among the tittle tattle with my free hand, I came across a piece of wood of around seven inches in length. I removed my tie and unfurled it.

"Now my friend," I said, keeping my voice as calm as I could. "I need you to be as tolerant and patient. There will be a moment or two of discomfort."

Mr Delphus of Clare's leg was as thick as my arm and I realized that a longer tie would have been much more effective. But in the end the crude splint was secured. Mr Delphus of Clare flicked his tail and clunked gently into the shadows.

25. Breakfast among a thousand watchful and invisible eyes.

MR SAMUEL BURGESS snatched another charred mackerel from the flames and chewed with gusto, turning to his side occasionally to spit out the bones. Mr Delphus of Clare observed with interest as the spindly arrows glinted momentarily in the air but, in his condition, he dismissed the idea of pursuit as futile and rested his chin carefully upon his wooden splint.

"You have made a good friend there Mr Durwood."

"He is a most impressive creature, of that there is no doubt."

Mr Delphus of Clare purred contentedly. Satisfied that there was no more flesh to be found on the denuded lattice of the mackerel Mr Burgess tossed it casually over his shoulder and, before it could hit the sand, it had immediately been snatched by a screeching swipe of seagulls. Mr Delphus of Clare raised his enormous head and chattered his teeth impotently but he was a cat who clearly recognized his limitations – particularly when hampered by a wooden splint – and was therefore content merely to register his contempt rather than enter the fray.

"I had no idea they were above us," I said, watching as the greedy gulls fought over the remains of the mackerel.

"They smell flesh Mr Durwood. Even from several miles. They make it their business to appear uninterested but as soon as your back is turned they pounce."

"How unsettling to be studied so intently."

"Indeed," said Mr Burgess darkly. "And not only by gulls."

"I do not follow."

"Look behind you. What do you see?"

I surveyed the scene for a few seconds.

"Only the cliffs. I see the entrance to the cave and our trail in the sand to this current spot."

"Look closer."

Even Mr Delphus of Clare appeared to have sensed some inexplicable force of danger for he now sat up in the sand and sniffed the air, picking out signals from a language no human would ever understand. But still I saw nothing apart from the vista of cliffs and sand. Palm leaves waved in the air, gradually increasing in vehemence as the wind picked up. The tangled forest behind them began to rumble ominously and I imagined the long path back to the village flecked in sunlight and shadow. Behind me, the vast desert of the Pacific crashed relentlessly onto the sand, each wave like a felled oak.

Mr Burgess studied the cliffs and the palm trees.

"We are being watched right now," he said. "Invisible eyes trained on our every move. Silver-maned demons. Picking their moment. Choosing their time. Which, I calculate, will not be until nightfall. Soon they will arrive in numbers and there will only be one means of escape open to us."

"And what will that be?"

"The sky," said the American, grinning broadly and revealing strips of mackerel between his teeth. "Allow me to show you."

26. A rare and unexpected display of devotion.

OUR JOURNEY UP the slope was relentless and, with each step, my breathing became louder and more laboured.

"We can turn back if you wish."

"No," I said, springing up from the bough and tucking the sodden kerchief back into my pocket with difficulty. "I am eager to see what lies at the summit."

"Very well," said Mr Burgess, still smiling. "In that case the directions are simple. Keep climbing up the path."

Eventually the path gradually widened and delivered me onto a verdant knoll which served as a summit.

"The highest point on the island Mr Durwood!"

"I am not...*surprised*..."

As I bent down, resting my hands on my knees to regulate my breathing, the American strode through the thick grass taking in the air as if on a leisurely stroll through St James' Park.

"What a sight sir," he said. "The ocean all its fearful grandeur!"

Clearly perturbed at not having elicited a similar awe-struck reaction he turned to me with a concerned expression.

"Are you unwell Mr Durwood? Are you in need of some water perhaps? Here sir. Take a draught from this bottle."

I am ashamed to admit that I not only snatched the bottle from the American's hand but that I also drained the cool nectar in less than three greedy gulps. I handed the bottle back with a nagging sense of shame but Mr Burgess had been distracted by something further back the path. He smiled to himself.

"You would appear to have inspired a great sense of loyalty in him," he said. "Most unusual for a cat."

I looked up and saw Mr Delphus of Clare hobbling up the final few yards of the path with his wooden splint dragging through the soil before it was silenced by the grass.

27. *In which I learn of the dreaded Hoopbelly and the unexpected benefits of polished bone.*

"DO NOT BE alarmed by the skulls. I assure you they are there for a perfectly legitimate and wholesome purpose." As I followed the American through the long, wet grass I tried to heed his words but, nonetheless, when I passed by a row of ten or twelve grinning skulls which had been placed on spikes at intervals of roughly three to four feet I felt my blood chill. Of course, reason and logic dictated that these grisly artefacts could no longer *see* or *hear* but, on this remote island, it appeared sometimes as if the rules of conventional wisdom in these matters were being constantly challenged by stranger forces so that now, as I gazed into the empty sockets where once a man's eyes had been, I was not convinced that they were entirely unseeing.

"Oh and watch out for the snakes."

"There are *snakes?*"

"Hoopbellies."

The American stopped. As he waited for me and the hobbling Mr Delphus of Clare to catch up, he stuck a piece of grass in the corner of his mouth and sucked on it, clearly amused as he observed me walking on tiptoe as if the ground was burning and with my eyes focused down intently.

"Not venomous, but still a critter to avoid if one can. They love it up here in the long grass Mr Durwood. They feed on mice and rats mainly but, judging by the various callouses and scars on my ankles I can attest that, unlike many of their kind, they are clearly happy to experiment with alternative sources of nutrition – even if, ultimately – such boldness results in disappointment!"

I gazed down at my vulnerable shoes, wet in the grass and easy prey for any hoopbelly which happened to slither by.

"And can they…bite through…*leather* sir?"

Mr Burgess leant in conspiratorially and lowered his voice to a barely audible growl.

"When we return to the cave I will show you a pair of moccasins which I foolishly wore when first negotiating these heights. And not only *shoes* Mr Durwood. See these breeches? Up here. These marks close to my thighs. The holes you see are also the result of various hoopbelly incursions for these cursed creatures are not only curious and determined Mr Durwood – they are also devilishly good climbers."

At that moment, had a mystical genie appeared from a puff of smoke and offered me one wish I would – without any hesitation – have requested the ability to float above the surface of the earth at a height of three to four feet and to therefore be safe from any hoopbelly attack. I had previously been under the impression that snakes were considered to be nervous and shy creations who avoided human contact if possible but the ones Mr Burgess described to me were clearly at odds with this conclusion. No doubt witnessing my distress, the American walked back without apparent concern though the long grass and laid a fatherly arm on my shoulder.

"But come sir. Truth to say they generally only hunt at night and so I venture that you are quite safe."

As I walked gingerly through the grass with Mr Delphus of Clare limping bravely by my side, my curiosity overwhelmed me and I was compelled to give it succour.

"Mr Burgess sir, could I possibly impose upon you for a moment? You mention that the skulls which we encountered back there fulfilled a commendable role. Would that be to keep the dreaded hoopbellies at bay I wonder?"

The American laughed.

"A most fanciful notion. No Mr Durwood, they have a far more dangerous creature to deter."

He stopped and turned. I stopped too – somewhat abruptly for it took poor Mr Delphus of Clare by surprise and he crashed into my leg, his brute force almost toppling me face-first into the grass.

"*Man,*" he said.

"*Man?*"

"Cannibals."

"I beg your pardon?"

"Those silver-haired devils from the village," said Mr Burgess, nodding in the vague direction we had just travelled. "Their lustful appetite for human flesh knows almost no bounds and cannot be diverted by any conventional military strategy as my poor compatriots back there would no doubt testify if they could speak."

"You mean, sir, that those... skulls... belonged to your fellow crew members on the *Great Plains*?"

Mr Burgess nodded gravely.

"As many as I could muster. I retrieved them from the pots at night when the murderous cannibals were asleep, satiated momentarily by their demonic feasts. My initial plan had been to confer upon the poor souls a mere semblance of a Christian burial for their paltry remains but inadvertently – and I must add, most *fortuitously* – I found that these immoral heathens may have been fearless in the face of muskets of bayonet or sabre but, owing no doubt to some peculiar superstition or fancy, the sight of a skull, once boiled and cleansed, proved to be as formidable a defence as a row of cannon. This happened one night as I was preparing a mass grave for those skulls back there Mr Durwood. Just as I was about to carefully lay the first head into the hole I was surrounded by a party of warriors and, for a moment, I was convinced that my bones too would shortly be joining those of my shipmates but then, at the sight of Sam Callow's polished skull in my right hand – a skull which I had

scrubbed so studiously to remove all traces of blood or tissue –
the scoundrels backed away with a collective gasp! It was then
that I realized how fearful these rascals were of polished bone.
That is why I have placed the skulls on the poles back there
Mr Durwood. Even in death my old friends offer me protection, almost as a form of recompense for having deserted me and
fallen for the transparent and deceptive riches of those godless
brutes in the first place."

Mr Delphus of Clare rubbed against my leg, his brute strength
almost causing me to lose my balance and topple sideways into
the grass.

"What exactly is it that they are protecting up here?" I asked.

"This," said the American, extending his arm and directing
my eyes to possibly one of the strangest constructions I had
ever seen.

28. The Eagle

"A KITE?" I ventured.

"It operates on the same principles. But it serves a more ambitious purpose."

Forgetting everything for the moment about aggressive snakes – I walked around the remarkable structure. It did indeed remind me greatly of the modest kites Old Jacob had constructed for me when I was a child and when he'd been charged to amuse me during the long summer months but clearly Mr Burgess was a man of applied vision who had transferred a simple notion onto a larger canvas – quite literally in this case because, as I stroked the material which had been stretched so expertly over the intricate and complex network of wood, I realized that it was coarse canvas from the retrieved sails of the *Great Plains*. Taking a few paces back – and almost tripping over the bulky form of the unsuspecting Mr Delphus of Clare – I studied the construction with awe. It now appeared to me as a giant insect poised to launch itself into thin air at a moment's notice.

"I am impressed sir," I said. "I daresay even the great Leonardo himself would have been pleased with such a creation."

The American tapped one of the broader beams at the side of the giant kite.

"It took a while," he said. "But after I'd had the idea nothing could hold me back." He spat out something from his mouth – which I took to be a remnant of tobacco – and walked over to me. "You see sir, I realized very quickly that if I was to escape from this godforsaken island then the avenue of the ocean was closed to me on account of the vicious tides and the unrelenting nature of the storms which somehow appeared to work in harness with the devilish inhabitants who occupy this place by always returning any defector back to the very spot from whence they came. That was when I looked to the sky Mr Durwood and realized that I had to exploit the strength of the howling winds which so often circled this cursed island. Realizing that the *Great Plains* was way beyond repair I swam through the shark-infested waters of the bay, retrieved as much canvas and wood as I could – which took several journeys as I'm sure you can imagine."

"Quite so."

"I call it 'The Eagle'."

"What else?"

I studied the American's creation again and tried to imagine it being launched up to the heavens from such a spot. We were at the island's highest point but still I remembered from my days back home in England how, as a child, Old Jacob's kites had often needed the aid of a significant run-up before gaining altitude.

"I can see by your troubled expression, Mr Durwood, that you are concerned about the wind?"

"Well...*yes*..."

The American laughed heartily and slapped me somewhat forcefully on the back.

"Look out there," he said, guiding my eyes with his extended arm. "See those rippling waves Mr Durwood. As a sailor I have learned to study them. A simple wave can tell you as much about the state of affairs of this world as all the charts and calculations of the most able navigator or scholar. Those waves out there are getting higher and stronger and the Big One is brewing. Out there, in those black clouds that are as heavy as cannons and which are aimed directly at us here on the only significant land for hundreds of miles. The storm is upon us and, when it comes, I shall be ready and the Eagle shall be ready. And you shall be ready too Mr Durwood."

"*Me?*"

"Why yes! You don't believe that I'm going to leave you here at the mercy of those heathens do you?"

I looked at the Eagle again and tried to imagine my terrified form strapped to its back whilst being tossed and somersaulted by a vicious gale. Against the vastness of the sky the construction suddenly seemed small and vulnerable and I imagined it being ripped to pieces like a raft caught on a tumultuous swell. The intertwined sticks and poles, so beautiful and carefully weaved, would surely be torn apart and the canvas could not possibly withstand a tempest of the kind Mr Burgess was prophesising?

"But come," he said, "it's getting dark. Best we leave before nightfall." He winked playfully. "We don't want to tempt the Hoopbellies do we?"

Having forgotten about the snakes momentarily my heart jolted and I looked down to my feet where the enormous form of Mr Delphus of Clare had decided to rest, his splinted leg carefully outstretched like the barrel of a musket.

"Come sir," I said, rousing him gently

We both followed Mr Burgess as quickly as we could through the treacherous grass and back towards the row of skulls.

29. A most eventful nocturnal episode

I WAS RESCUED from my horrific ordeal of being smothered with a thousand hoopbellies by Mr Samuel Burgess and his frantic shaking of the hammock.

"*Awake sir,*" he whispered frantically. "They have come. Just like I said they would."

"*Who?* What is…?"

Still somewhat dazed I rubbed my eyes and checked to see that the hoopbellies had indeed been banished. The hammock swayed and I clutched the ropes for safety.

"I reckon there must be close to fifty of them out there," said the American, his voice still hushed and urgent. "It's a significant war party and I can only surmise that the young villager you so valiantly bayonetted must have been one of their most honoured warriors and that now they are out for revenge. *Wake yourself sir!* This is no time for sleeping! Take the musket. It's loaded with the last ball. Only fire if you are sure to make it count. Otherwise use your faithful bayonet."

I took the proffered musket and my confusion was transformed into panic and fear as, outside, I heard the chilling war chants of what sounded like a thousand howling banshees.

"Are we to stand out ground and fight them?"

"Hell no! If we stood and fought we would both be in one of their pots before dawn, our bodies poised to be boiled until the flesh was as tender as spring lamb. We would end up like those unfortunate souls in the pot back there that I dragged and rolled from the village one night in the hope of allowing them a decent burial. Escape is our only option. Conditions ain't perfect. The wind ain't strong enough. But it will have to do. Tonight the wind must be our saviour Mr Durwood for, be assured, the Good Lord has truly forsaken us! Come man! *We must go!*"

As we ran up the relentless path I could not be certain if the ringing in my ears was caused by the wind or by our pursuers. Mr Burgess took hold of my arm and pulled me along, keeping his eyes behind me all the while.

"They are but twenty paces behind us."

"I cannot see them."

"You will feel their arrows before you see them. *Hurry!* And keep a tight hold on your musket."

I glanced down the path at the evil shadows of the palms and the other mysterious foliage waving blackly in the wind. We reached the top of the path and, breathlessly, I followed Mr Burgess past the row of skulls and into the long grass. I stopped and bent over double to regain my breath.

"What are you *doing* man!?" roared the American.

"These skulls. You mentioned that the islanders would not pass them."

"They won't. But their arrows and spears will. We are not safe yet Mr Durwood. And be careful. The hoopbellies are out at night."

A flash of silver from the night sky and a quivering sapling was suddenly created a few yards in front of me. It was followed by another.

And another.

I quickly realized that they were deadly spears hurled by the warriors. They had arrived at the top of the path and had stopped at the row of skulls but, as predicted by my erstwhile companion, they were now unleashing their arrows and spears with relentless gusto. The very air around me seemed to contain death.

I followed Mr Burgess through the long grass and – miraculously unscathed – we both reached the Eagle.

"Are you quite certain this will fly Mr Burgess?" I said, as an arrow whistled by less than two inches away from my head.

The American hurriedly uncoiled ropes and unfurled sails.

"The only certainty in life is death sir. But if the wind is right and if we catch the storm then I can promise you that the Eagle will take us high above the clouds and away from this cursed place. Now quickly. Climb aboard. And cling on to the poles. As soon as she takes flight we will be at the mercy of the elements and things are going to get mighty rough!"

I clambered onto the rickety craft and grabbed the nearest pole which was now wet and slippery with the rain. I gazed out and noticed a trail being left by an invisible crawler which seemed intent on reaching the Eagle. The grass parted like the Dead Sea and I imagined a horde of hoopbellies on the offensive. Mr Burgess was too preoccupied with the Eagle to notice. He wrapped the ends of one piece of rope around his fist, grimaced, pulled it tightly, jumped off the craft with the rope still attached and began to run though the long grass in the direction of the warriors.

"What are you doing sir?" I cried, standing up gingerly as the Eagle began to slide through the grass, rocking from side to side and creaking from a thousand joints.

"*Momentum* Mr Durwood! That's how we get this kite to fly! We need to catch the wind!"

I looked down at the trail in the grass again and discovered to my relief and inconsiderable surprise that it had been caused by none other than the redoubtable Mr Delphus of Clare! He gathered the last of his strength and leapt, the claws of his good legs digging into my thigh. Bearing the agony as best I could, I secured him in my lap, large as a young puma, heavy as coal and purring like the very thunder that had rolled in from the ocean. By now Mr Burgess had run too close to the row of skulls and I grimaced as I saw two arrows thumping into his leg. He didn't even seem to register the pain as, gradually, the Eagle gained the favour of the storm and the long grass fell away from beneath me as if the earth itself was sinking.

"*Help me up!*"

I took his arm and, as the Eagle rose up above the silver-haired warriors and the forest, Mr Burgess clambered up on board his craft.

"We *did* it sir!"

He whooped and grinned, seemingly oblivious to the rivulets of blood that were now pumping from the two arrows in his leg. Mr Delphus of Clare clung on to me for safety, his wooden stump tucked wedged in beneath a tight congruence of poles.

"It's the *Big One* Durwood!"

Mr Burgess grinned like a schoolboy, his rain-soaked face flashing with every explosion of light from the heavens.

"Yes," I yelled back. "I believe it must be!"

"It has finally arrived!"

I looked down. The once fearsome warriors were now tiny toys being submerged by clouds. The island's rugged coastline jutted out into the thin white lines of waves revealing spikes of secret coves and inlets. The full extent of the island's jungle and forests became evident the higher we got and, looking ahead, the ocean seemed black, endless and terrible. Like Death itself.

30. The Big One

MR BURGESS SNAPPED the arrows from his legs as if they were as inconsequential as sticks.

"What say you sir?" he shouted, patting me heartily on the shoulder. "Is this not an adventure? The Big One has been our salvation!"

Was there madness in his fervent gaze? I did not feel qualified to judge for perhaps I too had been driven insane by the cursed island which was now spinning around hundreds of feet below us. I placed my hopes in the fact that Mr Burgess was an experienced sailor who had survived many such tempests in his life and that, somehow or other, he would guide the Eagle calmly and safely either onto the peaceful shore of a nearby island or onto the mellow waves of the ocean once the storm had subsided. But to be truthful, keeping faith in his abilities was becoming increasingly difficult with every jolt and spin and turn as the Eagle cracked and snapped and dipped and swooped. I sensed unease in Mr Delphus of Clare too as he shifted in my lap and dug his claws in even deeper into my flesh but for Mr Burgess it all seemed to be a wonderful sport. His eyes were glazed – possibly fixed on some mythical and impossible horizon – his teeth clenched into a demented smile and with every violent jolt and judder which threatened the existence of our puny craft he would cackle and growl like a pugilist who was being perpetually punched in the face but whose pride and stubbornness refused to accept defeat. He glanced at me but I doubted if he saw me or Mr Delphus of Clare for he had entered a realm created only by his troubled and insane mind.

Lightning ripped the sky like paper.

"What a *joy!*" yelled the American. "*What a singular joy!*"

They were the final words he ever spoke for he was then snatched from the Eagle and sucked into a whirling vortex of cloud and rain – still grinning and still gazing feverishly at a tableaux that existed only in his deranged mind.

Poor Mr Delphus of Clare was next. Despite my best efforts he slipped through my hands and I was left only holding his wooden splint. I shouted his name to the blackness but he had gone. The storm gathered its might and shook the Eagle in its powerful jaws. Below, through intermittent gaps in the clouds and illuminated by fierce lightning, I saw the island spinning. Resigned to my fate I loosened my grip on the Eagle's pole, closed my eyes momentarily, allowed Mr Delphus of Clare's splint to be snatched from my hand – and then myself to follow.

As I fell through the clouds, spinning and flailing, my cheeks pushed hard against my bones, my eyes mere slits, my soul departed my body prematurely and observed my pitiful human form as it was tossed around and hurled towards its fate. As the island came ever closer, it was larger than I'd previously imagined. The jungle appeared to thin out and eventually gave way to a sizeable spur of arid desert. It was towards this featureless plain that my fragile composition of bones and flesh was now directed. My death would be quick and it would be as if Mr Hilary Durwood had never existed. Schoolboys would not huddle in their dormitories and read of his exciting adventures by candlelight. Monasteries would remain undiscovered. Would Mr Eustace Skate now forever remain unavenged?

The island was now merely a hundred feet away. Rocks and stones and ragged plants became clearer. Small creatures scuttled for shadows.

I closed my eyes and anticipated the brief second of pain before eternal salvation.

Departure

1. My thoughts upon entering the Kingdom of Heaven

IOPENED MY eyes to the Afterlife and witnessed an arid plain stretching far into the horizon. It was unpunctuated by any feature save for some dried and ragged plants which swayed almost imperceptibly in the breeze. Sitting up I discovered to my wonderment that my legs and, indeed, my entire earthly form was identical to the one I'd departed, even down to the clothes I'd worn. Raising my trouser slightly, I saw that I even bore the marks where the cursed centipede had bitten me on Lai Ming's raft. I ran my finger across the wound and felt the twin callouses of the raised skin. I concluded that perhaps this was the way with the Afterlife for, after all, had not even the Good Lord borne the wounds of his crucifixion when he returned and faced his disciples? I stood up, patted my clothes and observed that celestial dust behaved in the same way as its earthly cousin in that it formed wispy clouds which instantly caught the back of my throat and made me cough. High above my head a crew of angels circled in the cloudless sky, no doubt preparing to descend and guide me to the Gates of Heaven and to the Final Judgement. These angels were too high to observe in detail but I noted the occasional flash of white as their magnificent wings clashed against the light. Was Gabriel himself among their number?

I was suddenly gripped by fear. Would I be exposed as a sinner? As a vain and ambitious fool whose only thought throughout his short earthly existence had been the furtherment of his own fame and glory? At the Celestial Court would I tremble before Saint Augustine, the Venerable Bede, Charlemagne or even the Good Lord himself?

I sat down on a rock and discovered that I not only had a heart but that I was also sweating profusely.

I remembered about Mr Samuel Burgess and wondered if he too had departed his temporal state and entered the Kingdom of Heaven but there was no sign of him – or, indeed, of Mr Delphus of Clare. I deduced that the celestial realm must be vast and that perhaps my two companions from the previous world must have manifested themselves in some other region where they too had been delivered onto a soft bed of plants amid a desolate plain.

The sky was somehow bluer than the one I remembered from earthly life, bordering on violet as if on the cusp of a storm whilst the sun burned more intensely – glaring down as if its allotted space in the firmament was not substantial enough and that he deserved a grander and more considerable home. From St John to Dante I was aware that many great writers, prophets, thinkers and poets had attempted to describe the Afterlife whilst still caged and frustrated by their transitory human forms and that now I was in the privileged position of being able to witness it all for myself through eyes which – although hindered slightly by the sun's sheer force – were as clear and as focussed as they had been when I had been alive. Surveying the desert, however, as it stretched out for all eternity in all directions, I was forced to conclude that perhaps the Kingdom of Heaven was possibly not as splendid or as awe-inspiring as I, or anyone else, had previously imagined. Perhaps I had made my entrance in Purgatory and that there were various stages that I had to overcome in order to atone for my human weaknesses during my previous life before I could savour the bliss of Heaven? Certainly the croaking and cawing angels above my head appeared to be distinctly less ethereal as they got lower. In fact they seemed to have taken on the form of gulls and vultures. I deduced that this was confirmation that my life back on earth had lacked the necessary matriculation for automatic entry into Heaven for surely, if I had been a noble servant to the Lord and untainted by any ambition or self-regard, I would have been greeted by grander seraphs? Their less than magisterial appearance was now matched by a singular lack of grace and courtesy for they began to swoop down upon me, their wings a brush of warm and somewhat malodorous air – their squawks discordant and raucous. As their attacks became more intense I was convinced that this was a portent of my earthly sins and that the Good Lord had indeed sent these abominable and aggressive creatures to taunt me and to force me along a path to my Final Judgement.

In a brief interval between the demonic attacks of the angels I searched frantically for the merest suggestion of a trail in the wilderness but I could see no sign except for my own footsteps which had created unruly scuffs in the sand behind me. I was surprised that my celestial form appeared to have the same density and weight as my previous human incarnation and that I was able to create such marks but my puzzlement and curiosity were not allowed time to develop into a more considered deliberation for the maniacal angels resumed their onslaught and they were now so close that I threw myself to the ground like a sack.

These peculiar angels seemed happy with their work for, as I lay there motionless, they squealed with joy and circled, wings brushing against my back and their shadows causing quick flashes against the sun. I felt a sharp pain in my back and realized that one or two of these creatures were attempting to peck me as if I was carrion but, when I sat up, they squawked in cacophonous unison and flapped their enormous wings in something approximating fear. They retreated to the sky where, from a safe distance, they circled once again and taunted me with unmusical chants.

On standing up my surprise at discovering that I had created a vaguely human shape in the sand was compounded by the fact that my hand had been scuffed slightly as a result of my fall and that it was now bleeding.

It shone brightly as it caught the light but quickly dried to black.

2. Doubt and despair in the wilderness.

MOVEMENT ACROSS THE featureless plain became almost an illusion and I was often forced to turn around to check my progress. My footsteps in the sand were now swiftly erased by the breeze which had become slightly more forceful. To my left and right – and in front and behind – all I could see was a line of light ochre sand and dust cruelly curtailed by a block of blue sky which contained only the furnace of the sun and the squalling angels who persisted in tracking me. My shoes, once so finely crafted and sturdy that – on their day of purchase from Stroud & Winchester on Jermyn Street – I had wondered if I would ever again need another pair, were now as frayed as parchment, the leather flapping in thin strips with every step I took revealing near-skeletal toes. Similarly, my waistcoat was a ripped rag and, had it not been for my suspicion that the intense heat of the day in this burning desert would swiftly convert into shivering iciness at night, I would have discarded it.

The longer I walked, and the longer the sun scorched my skin, the more I began to doubt that I was in the celestial region at all. I was gradually convinced that I had, in fact, been hurled into the realm of Hell. Perhaps my earthly vanity and self-regard had been such that they had been deemed irredeemable and that I deserved to suffer in the everlasting flames of Satan's inferno? My naïve vision of this region had been influenced by childhood tales of flaming caverns and glowing red rocks but now I realized to my horror that the very heat of Hell was provided by a sun which, although similar to our temporal one, was a hundred times more powerful. Was it my fate to see and feel my skin burn like paper revealing sizzling flesh and glistening bone? Had the Lord forsaken me for my sins and now laughed as He observed my torment? Far from being angels, were the winged messengers up above demons?

As if they had somehow conjectured that I was pondering their constitution they began to swoop down from the sky, their wings outstretched and their beaks like swords. To my left, I saw what must have been the only break in the featureless sand for hundreds of miles – an old, dried stick. I picked it up as if it had been Excalibur and, shrieking wildly, I waved it around my head creating a pleasing draught but also, more importantly, deterring the cawing demons just as their beaks and talons were poised to strike. Relief was temporary for the joy of a spirited resistance and the prospect of battle had whetted their appetite for now they were joined by others and soon my little Excalibur, waving and whipping, was overwhelmed. I did succeed in occasionally landing a satisfying blow on one or two of the devils but there were too many of them and soon I was forced to run. Protecting my head as best I could against the incessant attacks I scampered across the sand with no clear destination in mind except the hope of a miraculous oasis or cave where I could shelter and recover from my wounds. But, peeping through my protective fingers, I saw nothing to disturb the sneering line of the horizon in any direction and, as my strength and energy dissipated in the heat and under the strain of constant attack, I fell down and rolled into a ball. I closed my eyes to await the deliverance of my second death. Aware, of course, that it could never come.

3. The two options.

WHEN I AWOKE my tormentors had vanished. I sat up and studied the skies only to witness a clear azure plain. Judging by the condition of my clothes I assumed that the vicious assailants had continued their attacks long after I had lost consciousness for now the material hung down like strips of papyrus and my skin was scraped and striped with dried blood. The sun was a merciless, furious disc and I would happily have traded my worthless soul for a hat. Never had I stood in a spot so unaffected by either sound or the whims of climate for the silence was so intense as to almost become a sound in itself – a ringing in the ears like a thousand distant chimes which, I assumed, could only be terminated and dispersed by a genuine sound, however faint – be it the scratching of a mouse's nose against a leaf or the distant buzz of a honeybee. Better still would have been the booming voice of Mr Samuel Burgess calling me over and then greeting me with an overwhelming hug or the reverberating purr of Mr Delphus of Clare as he rubbed against my leg and nudged me with his huge head. But there were no such noises in Hell. All noise and all sound had been expunged and sucked out of the world – if such a place could be dignified with the term. Similarly, there were no features for the eye to focus on and to offer the smallest semblance of hope. From left to right and in front and behind, all I could see was a dull plain of dry sand and tiny dispersed stones. I decided that I had two options. I could stand in the same spot and expose myself to the heat of the sun until my body – if indeed it was still a body – collapsed into a heap of bones crowned by a grinning skull, or I could walk in the hope of discovery. I allowed myself a wry smile at the enduring human faith in the concept of hope. Was it not hope that had dictated every move of my earthly form – the hope of seeing something new and sharing it with others? The hope of being celebrated and admired as a result? The hope of new challenges and commissions – possibly from Mr Julius Colebridge and Sons – and a row of leather-lined books creased and frayed as a result of being devoured by eager schoolboys hungry for such adventures themselves? What folly. If they could see into the Afterlife, those men, Mr Julius Colebridge and the schoolboys would see for themselves how pitiful the results of hope could be as they perceived with horror a broken man drag his ragged shoes across an empty and loveless land.

How long had I walked? I had lost all notion of time. Here time did not exist. A second became a year. A year became a century. The blinking of an eye took a millennium. Each step an eternity. My mind became crazed with the idea of water. Cool and plentiful. Gushing down my throat. My tongue was like a flap of leather – dry as a barber's strop. One splash of a raindrop would have been as precious as all the gold in Peru. I was already dead. I was nothing. No one. Forever dying. Forever without hope.

4. Intervention of the Divine

AT FIRST IT was a breeze stroking my cheeks with the softness of a mother's hand and combing away the sand from my matted hair. I closed my eyes in ecstasy and, had my body contained any water, I am sure I would have felt tears of joy tumble down my cheek. For the first time since my descent into the realms of the Afterlife I felt the merest hint of sympathy and was emboldened to wonder whether the humble acceptance of the futility of my earthly sins had contributed somewhat towards this relief. But my faith in an essentially benign domain dissipated as the breeze gathered force and, without any physical hindrance to check its confidence or hubris – no hillock, tree nor bush – it quickly became a tumultuous gale hurling sand, pebbles and dust into my face and impeding my progress in any direction. Once again my only recourse was to roll myself into a ball and wait for the cyclone to diminish but, far from weakening, the storm became fiercer. It was almost a sentient entity shrieking with pleasure at my subjugation. The sound was so extreme I was sure that, from that day on – whatever my fate was to be in this mysterious new world – the howling and wailing would accompany me long after the winds had subsided. But despite my misgivings, the storm did eventually pass and I sat up in a world which, if possible, was even stiller and more silent than before.

Gingerly, I stood and kicked my flapping shoes to rid them of the dust and sand. My eyelids were caked with sand as fine as soot and, rubbing them, I was momentarily blinded by thousands – if not millions – of tiny, diamond-like shards. Did I moan in pain? Did I scream? I am not sure. Perhaps I did but, even if these cries were emitted I was aware of the futility of any form of protest and aware also that I had brought this torture onto myself and that the only escape lay in a full admission of my sins. But who would hear such an admission? As my eyes became accustomed to the environment once again, I surveyed my position from the left to the right and from front and behind but, as before, all I could see was the featureless plain held down by a wall of solid blue.

I walked. There seemed no other choice. Movement at least offered the hope that I would reach the end of the desert. Perhaps I would see a patch of grass? Or a scurrying insect? Perhaps there would be hills? A village or settlement? And *water*? My body and mind were taunted by the hallucinations of distant lakes shimmering on the horizon. At first, driven wild by frenzy and joy, I increased my pace towards them – stumbling across the sand in my desperation and uttering guttural groans of antic- ipation – only to find that they evaporated in the heat before I reached them. Since the storm, my trust in the clarity and effec- tiveness of my eyes had diminished but I knew also that it was not entirely their fault for had not many a fine traveller been fooled over the centuries by the desert's cunning in conjuring mirages of this kind? Tempting and realistic as these illusions were therefore, I disregarded them and continued slowly across the endless wilderness.

And then I saw a spike jutting up into the horizon. Was this but another trick – another cunning invention to test my sanity? My initial response was to laugh and I wondered if anyone had ever laughed before in such a terrible and merciless place. This was not the giddy laughter of amusement but rather one of desperate hysteria. The sight of anything which disturbed the monotony of the terrain offered, once again, that most precious of commodities – hope – but, as the victim of several cruel mirages, I was aware of the fragility of that commodity and how it could easily be dashed. So I approached with caution, fully expecting the peculiar spike to vanish as soon as I got to within a hundred yards but, much to my surprise, the closer I got the bigger and more defined it became. With each tentative step the spike became more real and more defined until, eventually, I saw that it was an unsteady pile of rocks and stones. It rose to a height of around thirty or forty feet and I saw that some of the loose boulders at the top were in a continual struggle to retain their position against the forces of gravity and balance. The slight rocking motion of the structure made it almost appear alive – as if it was the neck of a giant lizard or a cobra poised to strike – and, indeed, when I was less than fifty yards away I saw one rock succumb to the inevitable and tumble down the side with a series of cracks until it thumped down into the sand causing a puff of dust. My eyes were drawn to the base of the strange pillar and that was when I saw something even stranger. There was a *man*. He was dressed in rags and his hair and beard were long and white. Pressed against the rocks and stones of the pillar as if held there by an invisible force his thin and bony arms were outstretched in a crucifix form. I sank to my knees and clenched my hands in prayer for I knew then that this was no mirage. Purgatory – or was it indeed Hell – had been visited by Jesus himself.

5. *A most unusual conversation concludes with a startling revelation.*

OUR LORD WAS naked save for a frayed sheet which hung from his shoulders onto his knees. I approached Him warily. His earthly burdens had persisted into the Afterlife for his face was a veritable study in anguish – His skin wrinkled and His features contorted as if He was still suffering the torment of the cross. His entire body was pushed hard against the peculiar structure and a form of divine madness had clearly gripped Him for, when I was less than twenty yards away, I could hear that He was mumbling words, speaking in a tongue I couldn't understand. His eyes rolled around as if in direct communication with a higher and mystical domain whilst the rocky edifice He was pinned up against rumbled and rocked, a creation as unstable as it was peculiar. Some of the rocks were decorated with mysterious carvings – cuneiform representing a once-living language which had now been silenced forever. I cleared my throat, patted down my torn coat and took a couple of tentative steps forward, my head bowed in fearful supplication.

"My Lord," I said.

But then my mouth and brain became as dry as the ground I was standing on for He heard me and immediately ceased his mumbling. His eyes stopped rolling and they tried to focus on what, for Him, must have been as strange a sight as I was to Him.

"My Lord," I said again, unsure as to how I should continue – or, indeed, whether I had any right to.

He continued to stare at me but did not alter His body which retained its crucified attitude. I noticed that His arms were little more than bone. His hair, gossamer thin and white as lace, hung down to his shoulders. His body was streaked with dried blood and bruises and I guessed that they had been caused by falling rocks and stones.

"You are...*real?*" He said. "Not one of those cursed visions or fancies?"

"I am real Lord," I said. "Or at least I think that I am."

"Come closer."

I approached warily, keeping my head slightly bowed.

"Put your head on my arm."

"Lord?"

"*Do it!*"

Hearing the wrath of the Lord with my own ears for the first time caused my heart to race and bound like a panicked hare. I did as I was commanded even though the request was somewhat unusual. I carefully rested my head against His arm and, as soon as I did, He reacted by wheezing as if in the grip of a sudden seizure.

I pulled away.

"Are you alright Lord? Did I do something wrong?"

There was the hint of a smile on His face and I understood immediately that He was laughing, or trying to at least, for He was very weak and every so often the laughter would crash into a distressing cough.

"You *are* real," He said again. "At *last*! At last it has *happened!*"

He laughed again. Confused but eager to make a good impression upon the Son of God – for I reckoned it might be of benefit in any future judgement – I laughed too. Then, as His laughter subsided, He studied me.

"Tell me," He said, "How did you end up in this forsaken region?"

"A centipede Lord."

"Centipede?"

Our Lord gazed at me for a few seconds and I realized that what I had said no doubt sounded ridiculous and needed swift and clear contextualizing.

"Lai Ming and his raft."

"Your tale has not got off to a good start. Try again."

"I was duped Lord. My naivety and trusty nature brought me to the point where I was twice betrayed – once by a crook called Lai Ming who left me to die on a raft with a fearsome centipede, and, more crucially, by an even bigger and more nefarious rascal. A fellow Englishman who deserted me in Singapore. I drifted for days until I was rescued by some islanders. And that's where I met Mr Burgess who attempted, bravely, to save my life."

"But you are now alone?"

"Sadly yes. Although I should naturally rejoice for Mr Burgess has clearly gone to a more celestial realm. Mr Delphus of Clare too I venture."

"Peculiar name."

"A cat. The largest beast you ever saw. With a wooden leg."

"I see."

The Lord groaned and gave me a disgruntled look.

"Tell me about this rascal. The English one you spoke of."

"His name was Eustace Skate."

Slowly, but perceptibly, the look of disgruntlement on Our Lord's face changed into one of seeming amusement.

"*Skate* you say?"

Unable to rein in my surprise I took a step forward.

"You *know* him Lord? Has he also been condemned to this realm? Did he fail in his attempt to reach the fabled ancient monastery at Pan Reng and perish along the way? I always knew he was destined for this place. If I meet him on this sorry plain I shall challenge him to a duel Lord, make no mistake. Failing that I shall pound him on the head with one of these rocks!"

Hearing this Our Lord groaned again and rolled his eyes. Perhaps I had gone too far in relishing such revenge.

"My apologies Lord."

"Stop calling me *Lord!*"

At that point a heavy rock tumbled down from the top of the structure and thumped into the sand but a few feet away from us. It caused a waft of wind which blew away the loose strands of white hair across the stranger's forehead. On it I saw the faint outline of a birthmark. It bore the unmistakeable shape of an Arabian scimitar.

6. *In which my admiration and adulation is made evident.*

SIR DUNCAN ROSEBERRY laughed raucously.
"And you really thought I was... *Him?*"

As he cackled I felt my face reddening with embarrassment and, in truth, with no little annoyance.

"I thought I was in Purgatory, or Hell," I said irritably. "As penitence for a life of vanity, pride and worldly ambition – a penitence I no doubt deserved sir for, as I wandered this desolate plain I have had sufficient time to ponder upon my shortcomings and to do whatever I could to admit to them and to attempt to overcome them."

Sir Duncan regarded me with clear amusement and shook his head as if in disbelief.

"Such erudition," he said, trying not to cackle but failing. "Have you ever considered the church?"

I took another step forward, raising my leg gingerly over the fallen boulders and rocks.

"My name is Hilary Durwood sir," I said. "I have been a great admirer of your books since I was a schoolboy. The number of times I pored over the episode where you discovered King Olhombora's ancient caves in Persia. Days and weeks spent on a wretched camel which spat at you at every given opportunity and which you were finally forced to eat in order to sustain you and your faithful and your diminutive servant Mamar."

"Tough meat, camel" said Sir Duncan, nodding as if he was conjuring up the distant past in his mind and re-tasting the meal by slapping his tongue. "Stringy too. Could probably have been improved by a healthy dose of pepper."

"Then," I said, taking yet another step forward in my enthusiasm. "Having trudged across the plains for hundreds of miles with Mamar on your shoulders as a look-out, you found the caves in a remote spot in the middle of a desert and entered them, the first man to do so for over a millennium. What became of Mamar I wonder? He is not mentioned in your book again?"

"A sad tale," said Sir Duncan with a sigh. "Essentially, once we had made it back to civilisation and to the port city of Al-dachamar Mamar accompanied me down to the quayside where I was searching for a ship to take me back to England when I committed the fatal error of leaving him unguarded for a few seconds while I stumbled upon an English-speaking captain and consulted him regarding possible passage to Naples. Renowned for their aggression, the albatrosses at Al-dachamar are notorious hunters and, because of his small stature – barely taller than a child – poor Mamar was snatched by the ravenous beak of one of the blighters whilst my back was turned. All I heard were his falsetto screams behind me, rising up into the sky until they became inaudible among the shouts of sailors and the lapping of the waters."

"A most tragic end. And somewhat unusual."

"Indeed. But one which was not entirely futile for Mamar had the ingenuity to take advantage of his situation by reaching for a piece of charcoal from his pocket and drawing a relatively detailed outline of the harbour and coastline. Forever ingenious and practical, the little fellow tied it up with some ribbon, weighed it down with a coin and dropped it. Fortuitously, it happened to land directly into the hand of Admiral Stuart Kelsey who was about to take command of his frigate *HMS Solent*. This map proved to be the basis for all further studies of that treacherous piece of coast and was invaluable in the war against France."

"An unsung hero for sure."

Sir Duncan Roseberry sniffed haughtily.

"Naturally, my publishers, Mr Julius Colebridge and Sons of Piccadilly, had their eyes on commerce and begged me to include the episode but I respected my friend's loyalty and feared that it chronicled too undignified and end for such a valuable companion."

"A remarkable coincidence!"

"And what is that?" he snapped.

"Mr Colebridge was also *my* publisher. Or at least he *would* have been had that devil Eustace Skate not abandoned me to my fate. We were to write a joint volume recounting our journeys in the South Pacific and our search for the mythical Tower of Ectha."

Sir Duncan smiled to himself.

"Mr Skate was clearly shrewd. He understood one of the basic principles of journalism and the literary life. A shared authorship is a shared glory. He wanted the money and the fame for himself sir. Don't you see?"

"All too clearly now Sir Duncan. Now that it is too late."

"Look upon it as a lesson sir. I myself was duped many times as a younger man when I allowed vanity to cloud my judgement."

I sighed and glanced around the endless plain that surrounded us.

"Sadly it will not be a lesson likely to provide much succour. I can forget any dream I had of glory or of discovering such lost treasures as the Tower of Ectha."

"But you *did* find it," said Sir Duncan.

I looked up at his crucified form, at his ragged clothes and wispy beard – at the faded scimitar-shaped birthmark on his forehead and his brown smile. I concluded that he was mad.

"Behold the Tower of Ectha," he said. "And behold also the wretched man who is *holding it up!*"

7. A great discovery.

"*T*HIS IS THE Tower of Ectha?"

"What remains of it," said Sir Duncan. "Once it was as magnificent structure rising up to the clouds and rivalling Babel itself. But look around you...er..."

"Durwood."

"Look around you at all the rocks and boulders that have tumbled down from it over the centuries. Some have long been covered up by the sand and dust. The ones we can still see have fallen during my tenure. Now look up. Do you see... er..."

"*Durwood.*"

"Yes, yes. Look closely and you can see that the entire thing is swaying, almost as if it was alive and with every movement it grinds away the ancient cement into powder, loosens another rock and diminishes itself even further. It is my fervent contention er... Durfield... that this is almost a deliberate and wilful attempt at self-destruction. The Tower of Ectha is tired and wants to be forgotten. To be buried forever and left in peace. But of course I cannot allow that. It must be *preserved!* However much of it remains I must protect! I must *do my duty!*"

"How long have you been standing there, sir?"

"Days have merged into weeks er... Durstone. Weeks into months and months into years. Sometimes it feels as if I've been here for decades. Sometimes longer."

"But your arms and legs! How have they maintained their strength?"

"It's most strange," he said, casually as if he was discussing nothing more unusual than an unexpected detour during a carriage journey from London to Bath. "But it is almost as if the rocks and stones themselves have penetrated my skin and formed part of my body so that my strength now derives from the building itself. There are times when I even feel more solid than its very foundations itself. But there are also times, which I am sure you can imagine er... Durwall... when I also feel as weak as a weasel propped up against a falling tree. *Stand back sir!*"

There was a sudden rumble from above and another rock tumbled down the side of the tower and thudded into the sand just a few feet away from where I had been standing.

"A modest rockfall," said Sir Duncan. "But still capable of damage if it hits the right spot."

"How did you discover the tower?" I asked.

"Instinct."

He shifted position a little – causing a small threatening growl in the rocks of the tower – and I immediately sensed that Sir Duncan Roseberry had been waiting for many years in anticipation of a moment such as this when, at last, he could declaim his oft-rehearsed speech for an enraptured audience.

"When a man has travelled the globe as often and in as many a diverse fashion as myself he develops a sense of proximity – a certain awareness if I may express it so. As soon as I arrived on this cursed island I not only surmised immediately that it was a place of unspeakable evil but I also knew that I was close to the mythical Tower of Ectha. It was as if I could smell it in the air. I had deduced straight away that the islanders had nefarious intentions and I had, like you had no doubt er...Durland... seen the ominous pot on the beach so I was aware that, from my very arrival on that inlet, they were sizing me up and judging how long it would take to fatten me up until my flesh was tender and full. So, spurning their duplicitous attempts at friendship I made my escape one night. Of course, I will now, with the full benefit of hindsight, happily admit that I had underestimated the thickness of the jungle and the dogged determination of the cannibals for the infernal devils tracked me for days through the undergrowth until I climbed the top of a summit and beheld a plain stretching out in front of me which seemed to signify freedom and safety. Indeed, the cannibals appeared to perceive this part of the island with a certain sense of awe and fear for they did not follow me down the mountain and soon I was alone on a seemingly endless desert. A man becomes aware of death. He joined me as I walked across the dust and as my throat became drier and drier. His presence was so strong that, upon looking behind me, I was sure I could trace two trails of footsteps! But the human body is sturdier than we know and, just at the point where one imagines it will snap like a twig it suddenly reveals itself to be stronger than the thickest oak tree and so it was that my hungry and thirsty body traversed this featureless terrain for days, weeks – who knows, maybe even months – until my instincts were proved correct and I saw the spear-like form of the Tower of Ectha jutting into the blueness on the horizon."

Sir Duncan paused and gave me a sidelong glance almost as if he was back in the Haberdashers Hall checking if he still had the audience in the palm of his hand. Seeing that he had my full attention he cleared his throat once again and tried to hide the fact that he had briefly been uncertain of his oratory.

"Of course, back then it was altogether a more *impressive* structure. A thousand feet high instead of its current twenty or thirty. If you had seen it in its full glory how you would have sighed! How you would have swooned! How you would have gasped in awe at the ingenuity and skill of the ancient masons and architects who had created this incredible and mysterious artifice in the middle of such an inhospitable region. Why had they done it? What was its purpose? No one can tell. Those secrets have long been buried with the men who created it. All we can be certain of ladies and gentlem–"

Sir Duncan checked himself with a sense of embarrassment as if he had suddenly realized that his rehearsed speech was being delivered to an audience of one rather than hundreds.

"Er– "Dur… Durl…""

"Durwood."

"*Wood.* Of course. Yes."

The great explorer shifted position slightly.

"All we can be certain of," he resumed, "is that this was a building of great significance within the culture that brought it into fruition for when I discovered it, despite the fact that it had clearly lain neglected and abandoned for hundreds of years, it retained at least a remnant of its undoubted majesty. Up at the very top there was a small cupola of sorts which may have served as a look out and, below that, a crenelated battlement with arrow slits. Arched spaces signified where windows had once been and where the mysterious occupants of the tower had gazed out across the desert, perhaps in search of enemies, who knows? Had these windows once been made of glass? Again, I could only surmise. All I knew for certain was that, at that moment – as I got closer – the tower was not as sturdy as it appeared. It was rocking as if caught in a breeze and, at its base, there were rocks and stones which had fallen away from the summit and the sides. Alarmed, I dropped my sack of meagre supplies which I had gathered from the jungle and ran forward for I realized that my role now was not that of the tower's discoverer but that of its *preserver*. My puny and insignificant body, already ravaged by my misadventures in the jungle and by the lack of regular sustenance, was surely not strong enough to repel the forces of gravity and time but I knew at once…er…*Durcott…* that I was its only hope and that therefore I should do my best."

He stopped and looked at me, abandoning his rhetoric and adopting a softer, more intimate tone.

"And that's where I've been ever since."

"A most incredible tale," I said. "And one which surely must be the basis of your next volume."

"My next volume? Sadly I feel that my fate has been sealed. No, I shall never return to England again. I shall perish here, my bones grafted onto the walls of the Tower of Ectha forever and eventually being buried in its stones as if in an ancient pyre."

"But surely something can be done?"

"*Nothing* can be done sir! If I move an inch the tower will fall and I shall die instantly! My life has been a full one and I have no interest in the futile pursuit of extending its duration for we all have our given share er... Durfleet... and I can have no complaint about the Good Lord's generosity when it came to mine. No, my concern is not my own life but the fate of this once magnificent edifice. My duty is to protect this once-magnificent building for as long as there's a breath in my body so that future generations can at least grasp a semblance of its power and dimensions."

"A most noble and selfless deed."

"It has little to do with nobility. The bald truth of the matter is er... *Durflint*... that I have almost *become* the tower myself. My outstretched arms are the beams that hold it together! My back is the stone spine running up what remains of its height! My entire flesh is turning into stone. In preserving the tower I am also preserving myself."

He looked up into the sky behind me and a look of relief lightened his face.

"Ah," he said, "here comes supper."

8. A strange visitation.

SHIELDING MY EYES from the sun, I turned around and saw a small black cloud approaching in the distance. It was a most unusual spectacle for, as it approached, it screeched and cawed and it soon became clear that this phenomenon was, in fact, a mass of birds of various types and sizes. Without any apparent fear or apprehension they landed around the base of the Tower of Ectha and I noticed that many held things in their beaks. Some had sprigs of branches speckled with berries of bright red and blue whilst others held what appeared to be scraps of meat or fruit. As the largest of the birds approached I could see that the lower parts of their beaks were full of water that they were eager not to spill. Any bird whose beak was unburdened by cargo stood around and issued loud alarums as if warning any bystanders not to intrude even though the birds were, by virtue of their panoramic perspective of the terrain, probably even more aware than anyone that there were no other living souls for hundreds of miles. With the well-drilled discipline of a Guards regiment, the birds took their turn in flying up to Sir Duncan Roseberry's shoulder and carefully transferring the berries or pieces of fruit and meat from their beaks to his mouth. They waited patiently whilst Sir Duncan chewed and swallowed before they fluttered down allowing space for the next bird to fill. This remarkable display took around five or ten minutes and I watched in awe for, in truth, never had I seen such closeness and understanding between man and beast!

"I can see that you are somewhat taken aback by my friends," said Sir Duncan. "And, indeed er... *Durlope*... it surprised me greatly too when it first occurred. But were it not for these wondrous creatures I should have perished a long time ago."

A large bird with a capacious beak not dissimilar to that of a flamingo flapped skilfully in front of his face creating a breeze which parted his hair and which Sir Duncan clearly found refreshing. The bird tilted its head and poured a generous serving of water into the great explorer's mouth before retreating.

"How remarkable!"

"Indeed," said Sir Duncan. "But perhaps I have grown accustomed to it and somewhat benumbed to its singularity."

The birds flew off in strict formation, from the largest to the smallest, until there was only one left, a grey twittering creature hardly bigger than a wren which held a red berry in its beak. It flew up to Sir Duncan and transferred its cargo into his mouth before tweeting a cheerful goodbye and following the others.

Sir Duncan sucked the berry for a few seconds before spitting it out.

"Sweet juice," he said. "However, I made the mistake of consuming that infernal fruit once. But never again."

9. An ingenious plan goes awry.

"PERHAPS IF I were to relieve you of your position."
"*Relieve* me?" said Sir Duncan with a snort of disdain.
"What nonsense is this?"

"Not at all sir. It can be done. I saw a similar procedure once back at Eton when one of the scholars attempted to rescue a tilting sapling from toppling down at the edge of Founders Field. It took three boys to slowly slide him away and replace him with a sturdier boy – Wilson, the Captain of Hounds as I recall – but the move was successful and the sapling was straightened and saved."

Sir Duncan Roseberry smiled.

"We are not schoolboys."

"But it can be done sir!"

Sir Duncan was clearly surprised by my enthusiasm. He stopped smiling and appeared to consider it.

"You really *think* so?"

Pleased and proud to have suggested a venture which had struck the great Sir Duncan Roseberry as being viable I looked up at the tottering tower and then down to the foundation, weighing up the problem and wondering how best to put it into action. All the while I was aware of Sir Duncan's eyes studying me as if he was almost scared that I might discover a flaw in the plan and disregard it.

"It requires strength and patience," I said, finally. "Clearly your patience is beyond question Sir Duncan but we must both muster up whatever reserves of strength we might have in order to execute this procedure."

"I am completely in your hands er... *Durcling*."

As discreetly as I could I examined Sir Duncan's weakened frame and tried to deduce if, indeed, he did have the physical robustness to see my plan through. What if his bones buckled under the strain? What if we both died in the attempt?

"Sir Duncan, I am going to edge up next to you and push my body as hard as I can against the stones. Then, when I am ready and secure in my position, I will signal for you to slowly move away. But we must be careful not to make any hasty or sudden manoeuvres."

"Naturally."

"Shall we attempt it?"

"Whyever not?"

I positioned myself tightly beside the eminent explorer and pushed my back as hard as I could against the stones. I could feel them rumble and shift defensively almost like a living entity which had sensed a new presence which posed a potential threat. Gradually, however, they settled into place. Sir Duncan Roseberry glanced at me sideways. His Christ-like arms were outstretched and his left now rested tentatively on my shoulder.

"*Now* what?"

"From what I recall with the sapling," I said, "Wilson sidled up to the less sturdy boy and then, when he was satisfied that the sapling was secure, he nodded for him to move away and allow him to take the strain."

"And you are sure this will work?"

"We can but try sir."

"Then let us do it."

I took a deep breath and pushed my back as hard as I could against the tower. Once I was sure my feet were securely wedged I outstretched my arms and prepared to take the strain.

"Now sir," I said, my voice croaking with the effort. "*Move away.*"

"Are you sure?"

"*Do it* sir!"

"If you insist."

Sir Duncan Roseberry unpeeled his wiry frame from the tower. I saw how the stones of the tower had left a seemingly permanent imprint on his back for it was rutted and lined almost like a map of a mountainous region. Freed from his burden, Sir Duncan Roseberry staggered from one fallen stone to another like a drunkard. He wheezed and grunted, his hands gripping the rocks as he slowly and painfully straightened himself up. His arms, for so long forced into their crucified pose, now hung limply by his side and Sir Duncan seemed almost surprised by their existence and uncertain as to their purpose. But after only a few seconds he began to cackle. The cackle turned into a howl and then he was laughing and jigging around the sand to some inaudible music.

"You are a bigger fool that I took you for...er... *Durlamp*! Look at me dance! *Look at me dance!*"

Laughing hysterically again he launched into an ungainly jig. But after a few steps – during which he had succeeded in enrobing himself in a cloak of dust – he stopped and walked up to me, breathless and staring me straight in the eye.

"I can't count the...years...I've been a prisoner...to this... cursed tower. But now I am a free man thanks to your... *folly*. And now I shall bid you farewell."

He turned and began to walk away.

"You are *leaving* me?"

"But of course."

"To *die?*"

"Look upon it as a sacrifice er... *Durclip*. By giving me my freedom you allow the people of the English-speaking world the opportunity to hear about this wondrous tower. I shall honour you by dedicating my volume regarding this entire bizarre venture to you so that the whole of England shall remember your name er... *Durflop*."

He patted me tentatively on the shoulder. Then, from somewhere inside his robe he took out a wilted flower and pinned it to my buttonhole.

"Take this," he said. "It is a flower hitherto unknown to me and, most probably, unique to this region. I admire its tenacity in persevering in such an inhospitable climate. Look upon it as a symbol sir."

He adjusted the wilted flower slightly before stepping back like a master tailor to inspect his handiwork.

"Yes," he said, patting my shoulder. "Perfect. And now, the time has come to bid you farewell. England awaits me! My Queen and my public. And I cannot disappoint them."

He turned.

"But how will you get there?"

"A ship! There is *always* a ship. As long as you are prepared to wait. And if there's one thing I have learnt in my period of captivity, it is the power of patience."

10. A mercifully brief account of a sensitive and intimate detail.

AN HOUR OR so after Sir Duncan Roseberry's departure I was overwhelmed by a surprising need to urinate. I responded in the manner that I would have done so normally in any similar situation where the location for such relief was inappropriate by clenching the muscles around my bladder area as tightly as I could and crossing my legs. Eventually however the urge became stronger and my muscles became weaker. I decided that there was no alternative but to yield. The warm liquid spurted out of my breeches in a series of curved golden arches and, as the urine formed a bubbling and steaming puddle by my feet I wondered if it would ever stop! The relief provided by such a relatively commonplace action was unexpectedly intense and I closed my eyes in near ecstasy as the liquid turned cooler down my legs and onto my feet. Such behaviour would have been understandably uncouth and disgusting in any other context or civil society but I reasoned that there was no other living soul within a good hundred miles and therefore I excused my action thus. I also understood that any movement away from the tower would result in immediate death as the heavy rocks would have been dislodged and crushed me in an instant. I gazed down at my feet and saw that the pool was being sucked in greedily by the sand until it soon became a dark shade. My predicament was somewhat complicated by a dilemma which almost immediately followed this one and was also of a biological nature namely the sudden desire to defecate. Once again, the recognized rules of social etiquette required that I resisted the urge until a convenient and private moment presented itself but – once again also – I realized that no more private a situation could ever materialize as the one I now found myself in and so, with a mixture of shame and relief, I relaxed my clenched muscles and felt the warm solids slither down the back of my legs and onto my feet. Turning my head away violently in order to try to avoid the stench caused the rocks behind me and above me to rumble in protest and so I stood as still as I could until the unfortunate act had finished. Almost within minutes the fetid air seemed to vibrate and, on opening my eyes, I saw a mass of black flies descending upon my feet and legs– creeping up and down my skin in a frenzied display of greed and gluttony. One or two ventured as high as my face and I had no defence against their landing on my nose and lips except to blow and spit but, on taking one particular breath, a couple of the insects shot into my mouth and I instinctively bit, crushed and swallowed them.

11. Sustenance from an unexpected source.

I WAS AWOKEN BY a sharp stab against my forehead and a sudden flurry of feathers. My attacker was a bird arrayed with feathers of red, blue, green and vibrant yellow. As my eyes became accustomed to the bright light of the morning I saw that this bird was accompanied by twenty or thirty such creatures, all gathered in a semi-circle on the rocks and stones at a safe distance in order to inspect this strange new animal at the base of the tower. Miraculously, no boulder or stone had fallen in the period I'd been asleep since my arms had not fallen to my sides but had somehow retained their position and my body had not drooped forward in repose. It was almost as if a mysterious force had somehow nailed me to the structure. The semi-circle of birds began to screech all at once and I suddenly felt as if I was the central performer in a play at Drury Lane. From their midst there appeared the bird I'd recognized previously as the one resembling a flamingo with the enormous beak. He tottered towards me, his head tilting from one side to the other as his large, black eyes took me in no doubt realizing that – although I was of the same species as the previous guardian of the tower – I was different in the sense that I had no long, gossamer-thin hair or tattered robes. I also must have smelled rather pungently although my ornithological knowledge was limited and I was uncertain whether birds were well-served by their olfactory glands. I saw that his beak was full of water. He nudged me gently with the tip of his beak to indicate that I should accept his gift and, remembering the earlier ritual with Sir Duncan Rose-berry, I assented and opened my mouth as wide as I could. The bird slowly tipped his beak and the water, still cool, trickled into my mouth, sloshing around my teeth and tongue like purest nectar. Closing my eyes, I groaned with pleasure and delight as it soaked the back of my throat and slithered down my neck like an icy snake before finally curling up contentedly in my stomach. Once his beak had been emptied the bird stepped back and some of his smaller companions approached me one by one and fluttered close to my face offering tiny scraps of fruit and meat from their beaks. I leant forward as much as I could dare – without upsetting the unstable tower – and carefully took the food between my teeth. Surprisingly, even though the meat was raw it tasted like the finest venison whilst the scraps of fruit were sweet and tangy. I wondered perhaps if there had been a grand feast at a distant city on another island hundreds of miles away where the hosts had foolishly left the food unguarded for a few minutes allowing the birds to fly in through the open windows to help themselves but I then reasoned that it was far more likely that the meat was from some fresh carrion and that the fruit had merely been snatched from trees at the very edge of the desert. Whatever the source of this most delicious sustenance I was delighted by it and most satiated after only four or five beakfulls. Then, out of the sun, a tiny bird – the one I had previously identified as being no bigger than a common wren – fluttered down and landed on my right shoulder. In his beak he held a sprig. On it was a glistening red berry which was clearly meant for me to eat. I opened my mouth rather hesitantly, for I had a countryman's natural suspicion of red berries and their often-poisonous nature and I also recalled Sir Duncan's ominous words of caution. But the tiny bird popped it on my tongue before my hesitation could offer any physical resistance. Then he and all the other birds flew off – their wings causing a brief but satisfying cooling draught.

After the birds had vanished I was once again assaulted by the sheer silence of the desert. My ears whined in protest at the lack of any discernible sound above the occasional whisper of the breeze and the soft rustle of a displaced strand of dead bush as it rolled aimlessly across the plain. The red berry rested on my tongue and, even without biting it, I could sense the bitterness of its flesh. Had the birds taken pity upon my poor and neglected soul and gifted me with a swift exit from this mortal coil? If I bit into the red berry would my troubles end? I prepared to spit the offending fruit out but at that precise moment the rocks above me grumbled and shifted and, in attempting to still them, I performed a sharp step to the left and, in so doing, I inadvertently bit into the berry! The juice from the crisp flesh was sparse but it scorched my tongue like a chilli pepper and soon my whole mouth was as numb as if it had never existed. This numbness extended to my throat so that swallowing became impossible and I was forced to cough until this task too became futile. As the noxious extract entered my stomach I felt the upper part of my body succumbing to its anaesthetic powers. I could not feel my arms and had to check to see if they were still there and performing their task of holding up the tower although it was almost as if I was watching another man's arms. Entirely unfeeling now from my head to my feet I was a prisoner to some invisible power which had gripped every muscle and sinew in my body and rendered them completely independent of my brain. Merely moving my fingers seemed as challenging as performing a full somersault. Somehow my lungs remained operational for I could still breathe even though I couldn't feel the air as it entered my lungs. Calculating that this was the direct result of the pernicious berry I had accidentally bitten I decided that the best plan of action was not to panic but to wait and allow the powerful poison to run its course. I closed my eyes and rested the back of my head against the tower. The stone scraped my scalp but I couldn't feel any pain. Soon all sound was banished. I could no longer hear the omnipresent whine of distant winds or the scuttling of rolling bushes. Even the ringing in my ears had gone. I tried to open my eyes to establish that I was still awake but I couldn't. All around me was black. My eyes were open. But I could not see.

12. The dented globe.

HOW LONG WAS I in this suspended state of Life in Death? Minutes? Hours? Centuries or mere seconds? It was impossible to tell for time too seemed to have become numb – the seconds and minutes and hours were as intangible as my fingers and flesh. But my senses slowly returned and the first one was smell for no longer could I detect the nauseous fumes of my own excrement or feel the dry grains of sand in my nostrils, instead I became aware of a mixture of dust, straw and leather. And *chicken soup*!

I opened my eyes and found myself standing in a loft room above the old stable at Havemore Hall. My arms were still outstretched although the tower was no longer behind me but when I tried to bring them down to my sides they resisted and proved to be as stubborn as poles so I gave up and retained my crucifixion pose. I watched as an old man and a young boy materialized before my eyes. I recognized that the old man was Old Jacob. And the young boy was myself.

"Excuse me," I said. "This is such a peculiar and singular event and please don't ask me for an explanation for I am completely at a loss as to –"

Neither Old Jacob nor my younger self had responded or reacted and I wondered if I was invisible to them. To test if this was true I noticed a pile of books on a table to my left and, as stiffly as a scarecrow, I swung my left arm against them but, instead of causing them to fall to the floor in a heap, my arms simply swiped impotently through them. At that moment however, a gust from the open window dislodged one of the books. Over by the fireplace and the bubbling pot on the other side of the room my younger self immediately drew a sharp breath of apprehension and looked over to investigate.

"What was that Jacob?"

I noted the trembly timbre of my voice. The purity of my skin. The innocent blueness of my wide eyes.

"'Tis nothing Master Hilary," said Old Jacob with an indulgent smile as he stirred the pot of soup. "Only the wind up to its tricks again. Pretending to be ghosts and trying to scare us. Let me close this window. No point having that fire if we leave the window open is there?"

"Are there ghosts Jacob? Mama says they're just silly nonsense and that I should take no notice but I've heard creaks in the night and sometimes the wind howls down the corridors and..."

Old Jacob allowed himself an indulgent chuckle.

"I've never seen a ghost myself. But who's to say that you're not a ghost eh, Master Hilary?"

"But how can I be? I'm not dead!"

"Maybe *I'm* a ghost! Maybe Mrs Murtle in the village shop is a ghost! Maybe we all died a long time ago and we never even realized it!"

"Stop it Jacob, you're scaring me."

Old Jacob ruffled my younger self's fine, blond hair.

"It's a strange world Master Hilary. Here, hold this spoon for a minute and keep stirring the soup so that it doesn't stick to the bottom. I've got something to show you."

"Can we eat soon Jacob?"

"Keep stirring. I'll be there soon enough."

Old Jacob rummaged among a pile of things in the corner, grunting to himself and pulling things away impatiently.

"Ah, here it is!"

Old Jacob struggled back to the fireplace carrying an old globe which had been dented slightly. He placed it down in front of the stove with a groan, stretched to his full height, rubbed his back and grimaced.

"Heavier than I remembered. Or perhaps I'm just getting weaker. Take that pot off the heat for a second Master Hilary and observe."

Old Jacob span the dented globe and the dust flew off in all directions, filling the air like thousands of tiny diamonds.

"It's been there many a year," said Old Jacob, bringing the world to a skidding stop with his palm. "I reckon it must have belonged to your father when he was a boy and he forgot all about it. Most things that are forgotten about end up here in the stable loft. Useless things that are no longer loved nor needed." He chuckled to himself. "*Me* included!"

"Is this the whole world Jacob?"

My younger self ran his little hand over the dented surface of the globe as if he could somehow heal it.

"The whole world as we knew it back then," said Old Jacob. "We know more about it now. See these large tracts of blue? That's the world's oceans. Since this globe was made there have been a few discoveries – islands both large and small, entire countries even – so it's probably useless now. Still, it's a beautiful object. Or at least it was until it fell down the stairs. See this dent in the middle of the Pacific Ocean? That's where your father dropped it when he was your age."

"I want to explore when I grow up."

Old Jacob chuckled contentedly.

"Do you now?"

"Yes," said my younger self, eyebrows knitted in agitation at his amused reaction. "I want to get a ship – I can go down to Portsmouth and get one, a swift three-master – I can hire a crew, a good captain and sail away. Then I shall write a great big book about my travels just like Marco Polo and there'll be statues of me in London and all the new globes won't have any blank spaces on them because I will have filled them in!"

"A most excellent plan Master Hilary and I'm sure you'll make a fine explorer one day. But for now I've got an even better plan."

"What?"

"Chicken soup."

Gradually the loft began to melt in a haze of grey smoke before my eyes and the voices of Old Jacob and my younger self faded before they vanished altogether and the smell of leather and chicken soup dissipated. Everything became black. Then I was aware of a glow. And of the heat of the sun once more.

13. I consider a permanent solution to my predicament.

A TROOP OF inch-long black ants had been attracted by a fresh pool of my urine. Some of the more adventurous among their number had crawled up to my groin and pinched the delicate skin with their legs no doubt pondering as to the source of this wondrous liquid and curious to see if they could somehow farm its flow so that it could be a more consistent element of sustenance. I was helpless to brush them away. I tried screaming but the ants were impervious to noise and a slight kicking of my leg – as much as I could dare without agitating the tower – merely encouraged them to bite even harder into my flesh for traction. To add to my woes I felt a tingle on my head and sensed a quick, scurrying movement. Slightly larger and heavier than an ant this creature moved on to my forehead and then cautiously on to my nose where I focused to the best of my ability and saw that it was a green ribbed scorpion which had been disturbed from its daytime rest by my kicking leg. It wriggled and squirmed to keep its balance and slithered carefully onto my upper lip where its legs struggled with the matted moustache. Its tail – armed with a cannonball sting – swung perilously close to my nose and I tried to move my head sideways in order to encourage the beast to crawl down my neck and, hopefully, down to the ground – perhaps devouring a few of the ants along the way. But the infernal creature had evidently decided that the tangled, wiry hairs of my unkempt moustache was a most desirable spot for contemplation for it lowered its body and adopted what seemed to be a position of repose. It tickled my hairs with its tiny green claws but then settled into stillness.

It was whilst languishing in this parlous state – with the lower half of my body being assaulted by vicious ants and with a venomous green scorpion resting in my moustache – that I began to wonder whether I might not do the world a considerable favour by performing a swift and permanent cessation of my tenancy of it. The most obvious means of termination was to simply step away from the tower and allow it to crash and tumble all around me. Even though the ancient tower was by now a mere percentage of its original height I calculated that the resulting cataclysm would be sufficient to crush me into a mass of bone and blood and that any physical pain from the process would be so fleeting as to be not worthy of consideration. But even though I took a series of deep breaths in preparation of this move I discovered that my fear of such a manoeuvre was overwhelming and not all of it was connected to any physical pain I might endure. I also felt a certain obligation to the once magnificent Tower of Ectha. The longer I stood there protecting it with my outstretched arms and stiffened legs the more I felt connected to it somehow, as if it was becoming part of my flesh and blood. I recalled what the tower's previous benefactor Sir Duncan Roseberry had said about it almost becoming a part of his body and I discovered that his words had resonance for that was precisely what was happening to me. Meagre and undernourished as my physical frame was, it now felt somehow bolstered by the stones that pushed against it, and the thin cement which still connected the lower part of the edifice was like the thin blood that raced through my veins connecting blood to flesh and to my very soul. My duty was to preserve it until a worthy successor could be found to continue the task. I realized that the likelihood of such a successor arriving was slim indeed for who in the name of sanity would think of venturing out into such a place? The island itself was a mere pebble in a vast and uncharted section of the Pacific Ocean and the desert, as I recalled, was surrounded by thick jungle populated by a treacherous and savage tribe of cannibals. But the resolve to carry out my curatorship was redoubled. I stiffened my arms. Dug in my legs. I winced at the pain of the black ants and, in a moment of instinct as much as hunger, I opened my mouth, bit the green unsuspecting scorpion in half, spat out the poisonous tail before it could whip itself into a defensive posture and swallowed the green ribbed shell, claws included. The tower had been the scorpion's home. And, strangely, it still was.

14. A reflection upon acclimatisation.

PERHAPS IT IS a tribute to the adaptability of man – both physical and spiritual – that, regardless of whatever challenges life may throw his way, he is capable of withstanding them and, indeed, of flourishing. By now, after a period of however long it had been – weeks or months – my flesh, bones and even my soul seemed to be strengthening rather than diminishing. Whether this was due to the regularity of the visits from the birds with their scraps of meat, fruit and water or to the fact that I had now developed a taste for scorpions and crispy beetles which I teased out from the crevices of the of the tower, it was difficult to say but, just as any clerk or scribe in the City of London swiftly settled into a routine and divided their working day according to its needs and limitations, I too had accustomed myself to my circumstances. Admittedly, being the custodian of a crumbling and ancient edifice was somewhat more unusual than any role a young clerk was ever likely to be asked to perform but, just as this hypothetical clerk was probably skilled in measuring his day by the subtle changes in the environment he saw and heard outside the office window – from the early morning shouting of the draymen to the late afternoon clatter of hooves and wheels across the cobbled streets – I too had developed a way of dividing the day into specific periods. Unpromising and unyielding at first, the desert had slowly revealed itself to be as varied a landscape as any in England for, just as the average oak tree in summer or spring proved a most effective gauge of the time of day simply by the amount of light that was reflected in its leaves, so the sand and dust of the desert revealed shallow, shadowy ravines and dips as the sun rose and fell. In the morning the landscape was often ribbed amber and black and even sparse plants glinted with pearls of dew. Then, gradually, as the sun's heat become more extreme, by midday these ribs and dips were eradicated, the plants were scorched and the blazing rays gave the illusion of humdrum evenness. By mid-afternoon and early evening the irregular nature of the sand was slowly revealed once more – although this time in a different pattern and painted in darker hues which sometimes gave the impression of greenery. Some of the mysterious symbols which had been carved into the fallen rocks were highlighted too but I could only guess at their meaning. Finally, at sunset, the sand and dust became dark blue and then, an ominous black which resembled the stillest and deepest of oceans. High above on the sky's endless canvas the moon gazed down at my predicament with cold indifference as, one by one and in clusters, stars pricked through like sharp needles of light until the firmament was as bejewelled as any king's cloak. As they winked and flickered in the icy night air I often wondered what those other worlds were like. So many blank spaces. So many dented globes.

15. The green berry.

THERE WAS A tickling sensation in my beard. Opening my eyes I saw a large black ant which had allowed its curiosity to get the better of it and which had strayed away from its fellows to the summit of Mount Olympus in search of sweeter nectar. Now its poor legs, so effective and nimble across the grains of sand and dust of the desert, were tangled up in the wiry hairs of my beard and its long antennae were waving in the air, desperate for any hint of guidance. As ever, the ants had been attracted by the latest pool of fresh urine which was quickly seeping into the sand. Looking down past the struggling ant in my beard I saw its less adventurous companions by my feet writhing like a shining chain of industry and urgency. A long black trail led to a tunnel which, I assumed, was the gateway to some vast subterranean city full of wondrous caverns and cathedrals. By now I had developed a certain tolerance to the bites and stings of the ants' teeth. At first the red rawness of the scars had raged with agony and I'd prayed for the coolness of the evening to soothe my wounds. But the night had brought its own tormentors. Millions of mosquitoes hungry for blood had been alerted from all corners of the desert and when they'd had their fill of blood they exited deliriously like drunkards from a tavern. I'd scratched the wounds with the soles of my feet until the warm blood trickled down over my toes. Having performed this ritual over a hundred times my skin had become as hardy as leather.

The birds arrived and, one by one – with their customary discipline – they hovered in front of my face and transferred meat and fruit gently into my mouth. The large, flamingo-type bird stepped forward in a rather ungainly fashion on its long, stick-like legs. Water sloshed out of the sides of its bucket-like beak. It stopped and leant forward, tipping its head so that the cool, life-giving liquid poured into my mouth. Satisfied that its work had been done it backed away and revealed the sight of all the smaller birds gathered in a half-circle. Some were perched on the rocks and stones whilst others stood on the sand. Many preened their feathers with their beaks as if expecting an import-ant visit for which they had to look their best. After a minute or so I saw a shape approaching and at first I wondered whether I might be a wasp or a large bee but I quickly recognized it as the wren-like bird which had provided me with the red berry all those weeks, months – or was it *years* – ago. Once again it held a sprig in its beak and on it there was another berry but this time it was green. The bird landed on my right shoulder and nudged me to indicate that I should accept its precious cargo. I opened my mouth, closed my eyes and sank my teeth into the berry's peppery flesh.

16. I witness a great battle and the pitiless desolation of the ocean.

I WAS UNCERTAIN how long it had been since the green berry had slid down to my stomach but now, when I opened my eyes, my body was numb just as it had been during my visitation to Old Jacob's loft. I was standing away from the Tower of Ectha and, looking up, it pierced the blueness like a spear. No longer a ruin it stood tall and proud. Birds circled the upper levels but even they failed to find the summit. I tried to count how many levels there were – three hundred perhaps? The stones, boulders and rocks were new and perfectly hewn into neat rectangles whilst the cement that bonded them was white and regularly distributed. Arrow slits looked out over the land like the eyes of giants. But what could there possibly be to protect in this featureless hinterland? As I asked myself the question the horizon was suddenly speckled by black living forms which, as they emerged from the dust cloud, I recognized as men. They were hurrying towards the tower. Some were on foot, some on horseback and a few drove chariots furiously, urging their horses forward by merciless whipping. An army was approaching directly towards me I instinctively began to search for somewhere to hide but the land was flat and I was horribly exposed. Sensing imminent death I closed my eyes but the army passed by for, once again, I was invisible.

As the soldiers stopped outside the huge wooden doors of the tower I could see that they were not as fearsome or as large in number as I'd feared. In fact they looked like the remnants of a defeated brigade. Their uniforms were torn, some were bloodstained and they looked thin and demoralized. Breathless and exhausted many of the men hurled their weapons to the ground and sat down dejectedly. One of the commanders leapt from his chariot and circled his bedraggled troops, cracking his whip and shouting.

"Are we to let them defeat us? Is that it? Are we to lie down and allow them to rape our wives, mothers, daughters and sisters inside this sacred tower and then slice off our heads to put them on pikes? Is that what you want?"

He kicked the soles of a sitting soldier.

"Do you want to die soldier?"

"No commander."

"Well pick up your sword and prepare to fight because if you don't I promise I shall rip out your heart with mine!"

Another soldier stepped forward. His arm was bleeding and there was a long scar on his cheek.

"It's no use commander. My men are tired."

"Tired of living Crtal. Is that it?"

"Commander, our forces have been quashed and now the savages of the coast are approaching. Soon they will be here and our flesh will be food whether we stand and fight or not."

The commander smirked sarcastically. He pushed his face close to the soldier, his knuckles whitening around the whip.

"And the fine soldier Crtal, once the bravest and most loyal of my men – Crtal whom the poets celebrate and the women of the tower crave – is now reduced to this pitiful specimen who stands before me, whining like a battered dog!"

The soldier called Crtal was about to reply but the commander silenced him by placing his hand on his chest because, in the distance, the thundering sound of an approaching army could be heard. The dust cloud on the horizon resembled an ominous rising wave. Many of the soldiers scrambled to their feet but seemed uncertain which direction to face or run to.

"Pick up your weapons you cowards!" yelled the commander, whipping the sand in his fury. "Protect your families! Let us take our strength from the tower! Heed the words our glorious ancestors carved into its very stone all those centuries ago and which have protected us from all previous attacks from these scavenging scoundrels from the coast! Let us take our strength from the stones of the tower of the god Ectha!"

I looked up at the tower once more and saw the lines of carved cuneiform translating themselves in front of my eyes. Whereas before they had been mere patterns and crossed lines they now were presented to me in clearest English.

"TAKE YOUR STRENGTH FROM ME. ABSORB MY ENERGY. CONQUER ALL YOUR ENEMIES."

The weary soldiers pressed themselves against the stones, closing their eyes and chanting prayers as they adopted crucified poses. After only a brief period of intense meditation the soldiers were rejuvenated and all trace of their previous despondency wiped away. Their bodies – which only moments earlier had been so bowed and defeated – now stood firm as if bolstered by iron rods and even their torn and tattered clothes appeared to be repairing themselves. This dejected army now formed two lines of seemingly indefatigable and impregnable battalions on either side of Crtal and the tigerish commander. Even their weapons seemed polished and new, the blades of the swords white against the sunlight.

The armies clashed in a melee of screams. Metal tore into skin and blood spurted in crimson arcs. Soldiers from both sides fell and the dust rose like a curtain over the scene until I could no longer see nor hear. The battle faded as if pulled away on wheels and all I saw was a wall of dust which invaded my throat and forced me to cough and close my eyes.

There was an intense bitterness in my mouth which was impossible to spit out. In my ears there was a swirling cacophony which roared and clamoured before suddenly diminishing into total silence. My body was now cold and shivering. Water surrounded me and the dust of the desert was washed away. I opened my eyes to see giant blue and grey waves rising like mountains and then falling away as if they were never there. Sizzling saltwater splashed through my body but never filled my mouth, ears or nostrils. Despite my stiffened pose – my arms still outstretched like poles – I did not sink. I walked through the oceanic wilderness as easily as if I was on a stroll across Hampstead Heath even though I was aware that the ocean floor was thousands of fathoms below. Huge waves and swells swept harmlessly through my body. Albatrosses cackled and squealed, carried by the wind like kites. Then, before me, I saw a body lying face down in the water and buffeted pitilessly by the waves. I recognized him immediately as Mr Samuel Burgess. His face was blue and bloated and I knew immediately that he was dead. Next to him was a piece of wood and I recognized it as the one I had tied to the wounded leg of Mr Delphus of Clare. I called out the noble animal's name but my voice was a whisper. An enormous swell the size of a hill rose up and engulfed me.

I was suddenly back at the tower, my arms outstretched. The sun was blazing and the roar of the ocean was gone. Looking up I saw a shape on the horizon. The longer I looked the more it resembled the shape of a man.

17. A most welcome visitor.

THIS MYSTERIOUS FIGURE stumbled across the stones of the desert, tripping every now and again in his clear excitement at having seen a landmark and, more importantly, another human being. At a distance of around twenty yards I saw that he was a young fellow of no more than twenty-five with long blonde hair that curled at the extremities. His frock coat was dusty and the buckles on his shoes were dimmed and scuffed but, despite the fact that he was obviously exhausted, his skin was healthy and the blond stubble on his face would, I surmised, soon blossom into a full and flourishing beard.

"Tobias Gently," he said, his voice strong and confident. As he extended his arm he smiled betraying a row of perfect, pearly teeth. "I am delighted – and if I may say so – slightly surprised to make your acquaintance in this god-forsaken wilderness."

Realizing that my posture precluded a handshake he dropped his arm slowly to his side.

"May I ask, sir, why you have adopted such a peculiar position against this pile of old rocks?"

"Are you real?"

The young man was clearly taken aback. He laughed but then he quickly realized that my face was serious and that this was no jape.

"*Real* sir? Why yes. In as much as anyone can be certain of their own reality I can assure you that, as far as I am aware – and I am told that according to the latest reports from the continental scholars the actual awareness of oneself intimates a definite proof of one's physical existence – then, yes, I am real. I am as real as that rock over there. Or those ants that are crawling up and down your leg. I say sir, are they bothersome to you?"

Clear concern for my welfare etching his previously unwrinkled forehead he searched the ground for some sort of weapon.

"If I could find a stick perhaps…or maybe a –"

"Come closer."

The young man looked up. He was now but a couple of yards away. Despite the fact that his apparel was dishevelled and dust-encrusted his body gave forth a fresh, almost citrus-like, aroma which would not have been inconsistent with that associated with gentlemen emerging from one of the barbershops of Pall Mall.

"Am I close enough sir?"

"Touch my arm."

Mild confusion mingled with a certain amusement on his face and the sun caressed his blond stubble causing each hair to glow expressing various shades of gold. Slowly, he raised his hand and rested it carefully on my left arm. When it didn't pass through my flesh and bone like thin air I gasped and my heart jolted as if I'd been a passenger in a carriage which had encountered an unexpected bump in the road.

"Are you alright sir? Your face…it…"

"I thought you were a dream! Another of those cursed visions. The ones caused by the berries!"

The young man took a step back. I understood his fears immediately. After walking long distances across a featureless plain in the hope of stumbling across any sign of civilisation – preferably an Englishman – his bad luck had been now to encounter a mad one!

"Do not be alarmed Mr Gently," I said, attempting a smile but realizing that my teeth, by now, were rotten and unlikely to promote a positive impression of my sanity. "It's the birds."

Tobias Gently opened his mouth to say something but then decided that he didn't know if his vocabulary was sufficient to the occasion.

"They come regularly," I said. "Once a day at least. The biggest of them resembles one of the flamingos from the Tower of London menagerie – have you been there?"

Tobias Gently shook his head slowly.

"A most magnificent collection. Possibly the finest in Europe. Certainly the finest in England. But that aside, this particular fellow – the one which resembles a flamingo – has a most substantial beak and he fills it carefully with cool water from some unknown oasis and, somehow, he manages to fly across this wasteland whilst maintaining most it intact before transferring it carefully into my mouth. Other birds carry pieces of meat and fruit and then, sometimes, a wren-like creature gives me a berry. So far there have been two, one red and the other green. Both have had remarkable properties, not dissimilar to the most potent opium, and I have travelled back in time sir – to the time when this structure behind me was over a thousand feet high – and also out into the middle of the ocean where I was pounded by waves and swells which passed through me like ghosts and where I saw the dead body of my old friend Mr Samuel Burgess although there was sadly no sign of the enormous cat with the wooden leg so, you see sir, although I can see the look of concern on your young face, you will see that I am not a raving madman."

I was slightly breathless after my speech and the back of my throat was dry. Looking up I saw that the young man was glaring at me with an expression of clear horror.

"Do not move sir," he said.

"Move?"

"There is a scorpion on your nose."

18. A generous offer is politely declined.

SWIFT AS A chameleon, I whipped out my tongue and snatched the wriggling arachnid. I bit off the poisoned sting, spat it out and crunched into the bitter flesh to which, by now I had grown accustomed and – much to my surprise – actually enjoyed. But as I savoured the snack, chewing, crunching and swallowing with evident pleasure, the expression of disgust intensified on the face of young Tobias Gently and he turned to his side and unleashed a strong, yellow curve of vomit which splashed loudly onto the dust and was quickly absorbed except for some curious solid lumps. I observed him with mild amusement as I attempted to fish out the last remaining section of one of the scorpion's spindly legs which had caught itself in the cavities of my rotting molars.

"You would be amazed sir," I said, sucking and pulling, "at how quickly a gentleman can adapt himself to even the most outwardly unpromising situation. Ah, here it is."

I spat out the leg and watched as Tobias Gently wiped his mouth with the back of his sleeve and approached me with the kind of smile I imagined he reserved for wild dogs or street robbers.

"Sir," he said, "perhaps I may be able to offer you some assistance in your troubled state." He cleared his throat. "My father happens to be Sir Reginald Gently, perhaps you have heard of him?"

"I am afraid not."

"He is generally recognized as being one of the finest physicians in England and now regularly consulted at Bethlem Hospital in London."

"So you think I am insane."

"*No, no,*" said the young man with slightly more emphasis than was probably necessary for me to believe him. "It is a common misconception according to my father that all the patients at Bethlem are..."

"*Deranged?*"

Tobias Gently reddened. He tried to compose himself.

"Whilst undeniably true, sir, that the reputation of the hospital goes before it in many ways I can vouch that the work my father, in particular, is involved in is of the most efficacious and progressive nature – work which is recognized as being crucial to the readjustment of damaged mentalities. I would be more than happy to arrange an appointment for you upon your return to London."

"Return to London?" I said, with a sardonic laugh. "And how would you suppose that would be possible?"

"Anything is possible sir if we set our minds to it. That is what my father always says."

"Perhaps, then – with respect – your father himself is the one who requires readjustment? Look at me Tobias. If I move these stones and rocks will crumble and the entire structure will fall. I will certainly be crushed, you too at your present distance."

A look of horror flashed across the young man's face. He took a few steps back but then immediately appeared embarrassed by his actions and pretended that he had been troubled by a wasp which I could not see. Then, after a few seconds of this pantomime, he sat down on a rock and sighed heavily, running his hand through his golden locks.

"It seems," he said, "as if we are both pawns trapped by a vicious queen. You are rendered immovable by virtue of that pile of old rocks whilst I am helpless in the clutches of our greatest ever enemy from the dawn of time."

"I'm confused."

"*Love* sir," said Tobias Gently, turning to face me and sighing once again. "Venus has me in her iron grip. I am not the first and I will certainly not be the last to suffer her merciless claws as she rips into my heart with each breath I take but such a vast companionship provides no succour, I can assure you."

"Perhaps it might be of benefit to you if you shared your woes?"

Tobias Gently stood up and cupped his chin in his hand as he pondered this suggestion.

"You are right sir," he said. "It probably will."

19. *A tale of great woe delineating the wicked nature of love has an unexpectedly fortuitous conclusion.*

"HER NAME WAS Penelope. I had known her ever since childhood when she used to visit our house at Latimer with her family – which was also my family for, you see, Penelope was my first cousin. As a boy I must admit that I never took much heed of this rather silly and effete creature who arrived each year to spend the summer months for I was more interested in climbing trees. Latimer House was blessed with a small wood at the extremities of its land and here I would often dash at the first opportunity to grapple with the iron-like bark of Lord Knowle. I can see by your expression sir that my comments have provoked a certain confusion – if not alarm – and so let me elucidate matters at once by announcing that Lord Knowle was what we called the highest oak tree in this wood. It was said that from the apex the whole of Sussex was visible and, indeed, on a clear day one could espy the murky outline of London or France and I, naturally, was eager to discover if this was true. Sadly my enthusiasm for attempting to conquer Lord Knowle was not shared by my cousin Penelope – whom I was forced to chaperone – and she was far more interested in gazing at the flowers in the garden and chasing butterflies with her net. But truth be told sir, as the years progressed, I made a most startling discovery."

"Oh? And what was that?"

"I discovered, sir, that I began to look forward to her visits. Yes, as soon as the summer holidays arrived and I was home from school I would spruce myself up, shave and change into my finest apparel and await her arrival. Oh, what excitement as I heard the rattle of the wheels as her carriage approached up the drive and when the snorting horses scraped their hooves on the gravel! I was in love sir. Hopelessly and indelibly. From that moment the world, for all its reputed hugeness, became a mere patch of grass no bigger than the one my Penelope was sitting on. All globes would have to be redesigned until they were no larger in diameter than a golf ball and the only country depicted was wherever my Penelope stood. I believe you get my drift sir."

"I do indeed."

"But love can also be cruel. As I soon discovered."

Tobias Gently sighed as if all the woes of the world had been trapped inside his lungs.

"I should have known that I was no match for her. How could I possibly compete when she was introduced into London society? Within weeks I heard reports that her beauty had been the talk of the town and that so many hearts had been broken after only a handful of dances. An infamous rogue from the navy called Captain Bonneville had proposed an elopement to Portsmouth where his ship *HMS Glorious* was about to set sail! I knew that something should be done and so, after a couple of days spent in abject sorrow I resolved that I should challenge Captain Bonneville to a duel in order to defend Penelope's honour."

"You are a *swordsman?*"

Tobias Gently reddened.

"Hardly. But I practised for a week every day at dawn using my father's old cavalry sabre. Then, satisfied with my progress, I took out Rosie, the fittest steed, and rode towards Portsmouth. My plan was to smuggle myself aboard *HMS Glorious* at night and surprise Captain Bonneville at dawn just before he was due to set sail. I would challenge him to a duel on the spot and, after a brief but brutal skirmish, I would run my corroded blade though his even more corroded heart with righteous fury!"

"And what was the conclusion to this grand escapade? Did you win the fair lady?"

Tobias Gently sighed once more.

"I was within less than a hundred yards of *HMS Glorious* when I was knocked out of my saddle by a swinging cargo and rendered insensible for two days by which time Captain Bonneville, *HMS Glorious* and my Penelope had sailed away. But that was not the end of my ill-luck sir. I was misidentified by a group of pressmen as an escaped sailor and the following morning I was forced into service on a frigate bound for the orient. The ship sank a month or so ago and I swam onto this island only to find it inhabited by cannibals! I ran for my life and now I stand before you, ragged and hungry in the middle of a desert in front of a pile of rocks. I curse the day I was born. For truly I am a man plagued by bad luck. My only consolation is that at least now things can hardly get worse."

"It is a most troubling tale, that I can concur."

"Sometimes sir, I long for those simpler days. When I was a boy, prancing merrily along the boating house at Eton. But your misfortune is just as great sir. I only wish there was any way I might be able to help."

"You were at *Eton*?"

"Indeed I was sir," said Tobias Gently.

"Then you will no doubt recall the story of the tilting sapling at the edge of Founders Field and how it was eventually straightened?"

"Of course. A famous incident. And a most noble pursuit. The sapling by now, I hear, is a fine tree. But why do you ask?"

20. A duplicitous manoeuvre.

"A LITTLE TO your left Mr Gently. Carefully. And do not be troubled by the falling stones. They are of no consequence."

Tobias Gently shifted his body.

"Like this?" he asked.

"Perfect. Now push your body hard against the tower. *Hard* I say!"

"This is…as….hard…as I can….*muster…*"

"Good. Now dig your feet into the ground."

"Should I… outstretch… my *arms* sir?"

"Not yet. Ease yourself into position beside me and then establish your strength."

"I…feel that…I have *done* that…sir…"

Tobias Gently's young face was slowly turning purple with the effort but, gradually, his breathing regulated itself and, having secured his stance, he turned to me, nodded and tried his best to smile.

"Good," I said. "Now I am slowly about to move away from the tower. Are you content to take the weight?"

"I…*think* so…"

Carefully, like a man being released from a prison cell – and feeling peculiarly terrified at the prospect of his new-found freedom being suddenly snatched away from him at the final moment – I stepped away from my burden. All at once my body felt as ethereal as a cloud and I was fearful in case I should suddenly float up helplessly into the sky unless I picked up one of the stones as a counterweight. Bending down to pick one up was a relatively simple act but, for someone who had been trapped in a crucifix pose for what had seemed like an eternity, reaching for a stone and rolling it in my hands caused me to laugh out loud in a paroxysm of joy and provoked a merry jig as I hopped from one foot to another like a fool! Even the air felt sweeter. Closing my eyes in ecstasy I allowed it to swell up my lungs and held it prisoner for as long as I dared until allowing the slow and delicious process of release.

"I feel that the...stones...are...*moving*..."

Jolted back into the real world by the sound of Tobias Gently's strained tones I turned to face him.

"Keep your arms outstretched sir," I said. "As stiff as you can manage."

"For how...*long*...sir?"

I smiled.

"There is no doubt that, at first, it will feel as if your whole body is about to buckle and break."

"I believe I am at...that stage...*now*..."

Still smiling, I took a few steps in his direction.

"Gradually, in time, you will discover a strength – an inner strength which I am convinced comes directly from the stones of the tower themselves. It is an ancient power – mysterious and, quite possibly, immune to any scientific enquiry."

"*Gradually?*" said the young man, the initial strains of holding up the tower etching wrinkles and lines in his soft skin like a cruel knife. "You said...*gradually*...sir...and...*in time?*"

"Indeed so."

"You intend to...*leave* me here?"

"Ungentlemanly I grant you."

Anger now joined forces with pain on the young man's face.

"You...*tricked* me you knave!"

The spittle from his outrage speckled my face. I wiped it away with the back of my hand. Moving as if to try to strangle me, Tobias Gently was immediately halted by the unstable rumble of the rocks above his head and, much to his fury, he was forced to remain impotently crucified to the tower.

"I will get my...*revenge*...sir..."

"I can only apologize Mr Gently. I agree that it is an under-hand act and not one that I am especially proud of. I have no doubt that, one day, you too, despite your youthful nobility and highly developed sense of justice, will also be forced to stoop to such deception. It is a wicked world. Unfair, cruel and servile to the whims of crooks. To control it so that it conforms with our wishes we must sometimes sacrifice our ideals and principles. Goodbye sir. I have my own act of revenge to pursue."

As I stepped back and turned to go Tobias Gently raised his voice and struggled like a mad dog against the invisible leash which held him to the rumbling tower.

"*You are leaving me to die!*"

"The birds will come," I said, facing him for the last time. "They always have done it seems. They will sustain you."

"Murderer! Curse you! I will have my revenge! *Murderer!!*"

Tobias Gently's cries and screams became more muted as I walked away from the Tower of Ectha. In time they were no more than a whisper. Smothered by the wind and the gentle rush of the ocean. Then they were gone forever.

Return

1. The tragic and horrific death of Mary Braggan.

"'E'S RETURNED I tell you! Satan 'as returned! Straight from the bowels of Hell to take revenge and who can blame 'im? Not me. I've been sayin' it for years I 'ave. Mind your evil ways I said. 'E will come up an' 'e'll strike you down sure as I'm standin' 'ere beside you! 'Ere, what's 'e doin' with that pencil?"

"Madam, allow me."

I placed a tentative arm on the old landlady's shawl and led her away to a corner, raising an eyebrow to Harry Bunch as I passed. Bunch merely shrugged and continued with his sketching.

"Funny line o' business if you ask me," she said, nodding in the direction of my partner. "'Oo'd want to draw a dead body?"

"Did you know her well?"

"Oo?"

I nodded over my shoulder to indicate the corpse. The old lady drew in her toothless gums, scraped her throat and spat out a whip of phlegm.

"I knew her alright. Slattern she was. Mary Braggan. That was 'er name. The devil's own daughter if you ask me. Always daan the Nag and comin' 'ome with a different trick each night. Wrong sort too. Not gentlemen. Not like you with yer nice manners. Wouldn't 've been so bad if they 'ad been gentlemen. But they wasn't gentlemen. *Pigs.* And one of 'em did for 'er. Well I ain't cryin' no crocodile tears for 'er that's for sure. You can write that daan in yer notebook for all the good it'll do. She deserved all she 'ad comin'. You got that? You written that daan? Cos I don't see you writin' nothin'."

"Did you see what happened last night Mrs Cratham?"

She sucked in her gums until her mouth was a thin and crooked line. For a moment I thought she was going to spit again but she decided against it.

"I 'eard the scream. I 'eard that alright. Thought it was a fox. You get lots of them round 'ere. Mangy they are. Covered in fleas. Anyways, I looked out the winder but couldn't see nuthin' so I goes back to bed and only saw her this mornin' when I went out the back. I wondered what all the flies were about. And the cats. Licking away the blood they were. Little bastards! They scarpered when I got the broom out!" She cackled like a witch revealing pink and yellow gums. "'Ere, you writin' any of this down?"

I scrambled for my notebook and pencil.

"Yes. Yes of course."

I wrote down the word *cats*.

"Is that all you gonna write? I mean, I can't read no good but I know 'ow long it takes to write a sentence and that was no sentence. I'm no fool. Got no schooling but I ain't no fool. What was your name again?"

"Hilary Durwood."

"Girl's name innit?"

I licked the tip of my pencil.

"Have you got any other lodgers at the moment Mrs Cratham?"

"Only Mr Barrett."

"And he's not in?"

"Works in an office 'e does. Comes 'ome with lots of books under 'is arm. Work 'im down to the ground they do. Poor soul. I try to fatten him up but 'e's as thin as a rod, 'is poor mother would be worried if she wasn't already dead."

"No knives missing from the kitchen or anything?"

"'Ere, you one o' them detectives?"

"Just a journalist."

Mrs Cratham snorted, turned her head and spat into the corner. "Pretty words ain't gonna catch the one 'oo did it. Not that the Peelers stand a chance either mind. Not unless they got shovels big enough to dig down all the way to Hell. 'Cos I tell you, Satan 'imself cut her up! No 'uman could do that. It's either Satan or the Slasher."

Mrs Cratham stopped in full flow, clearly struck by a thought. She leant in and lowered her voice.

"'Ere, do you think it was 'im do ya?"

"*Satan?* I doubt it."

Mrs Cratham growled disapproval at my words.

"Idiot!"

She lowered her voice until it was no more than a whisper and looked around the back yard as if checking there was no one else within earshot.

"I meant *The Slasher*. Reckon it was 'im?"

"Well, all his victims so far have been south of the river and within a very specific area. There haven't been any reports of any such killings round here."

"You've seen 'er though 'ilary! Mary Braggan! You've seen what 'e did. Her guts 'angin' out. Throat ripped apart. I tell you Mr Durwood, if it ain't Satan what done that it could only be The Slasher."

She peered over my shoulder.

"What's takin' 'im so long? How long could it take to draw a dead body?"

"He's a perfectionist Mrs Cratham."

"Yeah well, I knew his mother. Lydia Bunch. And a right slut she was too. I remember 'im runnin' round in his mucky breeches so I 'ope 'e doesn't think he can cone round 'ere and lord it over me."

"I'm sure he wouldn't dream of it Mrs Cratham. Ah, here he comes."

"Right," said Harry Bunch, tucking the notebook and pen into his inside pocket. "Let's go before the Peelers come back."

He turned to the old landlady and doffed his hat.

"Thank you very much for your time Mrs Cratham," he said, raising his voice a little for her benefit.

Mrs Cratham growled her discontent and spat into the corner.

"Little shit."

2. The curiosity of Mr Harry Bunch elicits a lie.

"SHE TOLD ME that you grew up around here."
Harry Bunch settled in his chair, sipped his porter, wiped the foam off his moustache with his sleeve and smiled.

"Old crow. Ancient as the hills she was then too. God only knows how old she is now. Five hundred at least."

I sipped my porter too although I had yet to acquire an enthusiasm for its rather cloying bitterness. I attempted to hide my lack of appreciation by holding the tankard up to my lips as I swallowed and winced.

"I was just a nipper," said Harry Bunch. "But I always remember her shrieking like a banshee at everyone. My dear old mother too – God rest her soul – would get dragged in. Once I remember they had a right old ding dong. Out in the street it was – just round the corner from here. Some words were spoken and my mother got her temper up and grabbed the old sow's hair until she squealed. After that she used to throw things at me if she ever caught me walking past her house in the back alley. Chunks of old stinking cheese. Bones. Broken cups. Anything she could lay her hands on. I wasn't sure if she'd recognise me after all these years. Not with the moustache and the hat. But she's clearly got the memory of an elephant. Skin of one too if you ask me!"

He gulped at his porter and released a sigh of satisfaction.

"At least we caught the Peelers on the hop," he said. "They never thought the Slasher would strike north of the river. We would never 've got a look in otherwise. They'd 've run us off threatening jail and all that."

"They would actually do that?"

"Happened a lot with my old partner Mayfield when we were on the trail of that kid murderer in Stepney a few years back. Nasty affair that was. Still. They caught him in the end. Chap called Kendall. Hanged him at Newgate. Big crowd that day but me and Mayfield were there in the front row. Got a good sketch. Managed to get a good one just now of little Mary Braggan too. What d' you reckon?"

Harry Bunch took out his sketch book, wiped the table with his elbow, laid the book out on the table and flattened out the pages. After only a few weeks of partnership I had come to realize that my colleague, despite his lack of formal training, was a singularly gifted draughtsman. His pencil had skilfully traced the full horror of the scene in Mrs Cratham's back yard – the way poor Mary Braggan's body had been ripped open like a pea pod and the way her face seemed almost serene, as if she was sleeping peacefully whilst her innards had tumbled out all around her like obscene bedding. I sipped some of the foam from my porter.

"Have you ever considered applying to the Royal Academy Mr Bunch?"

Harry Bunch closed the sketch book and tucked it into his inside pocket before clicking his fingers to attract the landlord's attention and indicating that another two porters were required at our table. The landlord nodded and awoke his half-sleeping pump boy with a sharp kick to his backside.

"The likes of me don't get into places like the Academy. That's reserved for gentlemen. Like yourself."

"We live in enlightened times Mr Bunch. The doors of our great institutions are open to all who have the requisite gifts, regardless of class or financial considerations."

"Spoken like a true gentleman if I may say so," said Harry Bunch. "Because only a true gentleman could believe for a minute that any of that was true."

"But surely –"

"Drink up Durwood. You're falling behind."

The pump boy carefully took the two tankards of fresh porter from the tray and laid them on the table. As Harry Bunch had correctly deduced, my original tankard was still three-quarters full and draining the remainder of it was not a prospect which filled me with any great delight. My stomach was already churning after witnessing the torn and corrupted form of Mary Braggan and now the porter was uniting with this vision to create a most uncomfortable tumult which I felt could erupt unexpectedly at any moment resulting in widespread embarrassment and shame. However, not wishing to appear impolite, I closed my eyes and filled my mouth with the evil-tasting tincture before swallowing as quickly as I could. I wiped my mouth and tried not to think too hard about the next tankard of porter which was in front of me – the foam spilling over the sides and forming a bubbling pool on the table. I was aware of Harry Bunch's stare.

"You intrigue me," he said, finally.

"I'm not sure if I warrant such curiosity."

I tried a light-hearted laugh but Harry Bunch did not reciprocate. He smiled like an interrogator who appeared to be in possession of some secret knowledge.

"I've been in this game for a while. It's a decent life. They pay me for what I do and I do a good job. Beats working down by the river or breaking my back in some workhouse. But you Hilary…"

He studied my face as if preparing mentally for a portrait – taking in all the pits and contours of my bones and skin.

"You are a proper gentleman. No amount of ragged hair or broken teeth can disguise it. The minute we were paired up I thought to myself 'hello, this fellow is different to old Mayfield'."

"I'm sure I'm not all that different."

I sipped the vile porter.

"Oh but you are Hilary. A proper gent. The way you talk. The way you conduct yourself. A proper gent. You can't hide good breeding."

I continued to sip the bitter porter.

Harry Bunch leant forward.

"So tell me. What's the story?"

"Story?"

Harry Bunch smiled.

"Must be one hell of a story if you ask me. Something must have happened to drag a gentleman like yourself down to these murky backwaters of life."

"Well, I…"

"I know what it was."

My heart began to thump.

"Do you?"

Harry Bunch wagged his finger as he continued smiling. He leant forward even further and lowered his voice.

"It was a *woman* wasn't it?"

I had a vision of The Tower of Ectha. Of Tobias Gently as a skeleton around the base. Rocks and stones everywhere. Vultures circling.

I nodded.

"I *knew* it!" said Harry Bunch.

He clapped his hands in delight so loudly that the landlord and his boy looked across. But Harry Bunch was unconcerned.

"What was her name?"

"Penelope."

"What else?" said Harry Bunch, smiling. "She *would* be called Penelope wouldn't she? *Hilary* and *Penelope*. A true lady for a true gentleman. What happened? Break your heart did she?"

I avoided his eye and tried to sigh as convincingly as I could.

"She ran away. Eloped with another man. Someone considerably more dashing than myself. Of course I chased after her but to no avail. And now I shall never see her again."

I allowed myself a sly sideways glance to see if Harry Bunch had believed me. It was difficult to tell. He was still nodding and smiling.

"Heard it many times before my friend. So let me guess. You ran up debts, you gambled away your fortune and now that you're on your uppers you're forced into this game just to keep body and soul together."

"Indeed."

"She must've been some beauty?"

"She was."

"Blonde?"

"Like gold."

"Ringlets?"

"So perfect they almost jingled."

"Played the pianoforte like an angel?"

"Sang too."

Harry Bunch raised his tankard and invited me to clink it in a toast. Which I did.

"To Penelope," he said. "Her loss is London's gain."

He finished off the porter in a series of greedy gulps before crashing the tankard down on the table with impressive finality.

3. A letter home.

Islington, March 23.

My dear Father,

How delightful and pleasant it was to be back at Havemore Hall again last week and to once again be by your bedside. Doctor Bellwether has clearly made excellent work in the promotion of your well-being and the medications he has prepared appear to have been most effective. When Rosie brought in the tea it was heartening to see you sitting up in bed without her aid and nibbling one of the biscuits since – and I am sure that Rosie would not mind my breaking her confidentiality in this matter – I gleaned from her afterwards that a mere fortnight ago the prospect of savouring one of Mrs Bartlett's spiced ginger cracknells would have been a task of near-insurmountable difficulty! Father, whilst I am engaged in expressions of gladness and pleasure allow me also to state how overjoyed I was also when I took an opportunity after our conversation to stroll around the garden and grounds and discovered that they presented such a charming and enchanting aspect. Old Jacob would surely have been gladdened by the work of the new man – Hewlett is it? I am afraid I didn't catch the fellow's name and although I could see his shape in the distance and waved my arms to catch his attention I fear that he may not have seen or recognized me. Old Jacob's grave has been well-tended and I shed a tear as I lay down a few modest flowers. He was such a fine fellow and will forever be in my thoughts. I sat there for hours at the grave, never even caring that the wet soil was seeping into my breeches, savouring the peace. Enjoying the chirping birds. Some of them came down from the trees and brushed their tiny beaks against my hand. One allowed itself to be cupped in my hand until I released it into the air once again. Old Jacob would have surely been astounded at such a development but, following my travels, I myself have ceased to be surprised by the actions of birds or, indeed, of nature in general.

Father, I understand entirely how distressed you were upon witnessing my physical condition when I first walked up to your bedside after such a long absence from England but I wanted to assure you that, despite my depleted form and the fact that I had lost the odd tooth, I am strong and resolute and another fact that I have gleaned from my travels is that the human form can withstand astounding levels of punishment and torture and still endure. You will no doubt be pleased to learn that when I returned from my stroll around the grounds Mrs Bartlett conjured up a wondrous lamb stew with some of her home baked bread and winked at me as she placed a rather fine Bordeaux on the table saying she was sure the master wouldn't disapprove seeing as it was such a special occasion! I believe it was the 1814 but was assured that there were two others nestling in the furthest reaches of the cellar in readiness for Christmas. Mrs Bartlett also kindly took a pair of scissors to my long and straggly hair – to be truthful I had forgotten how long it had become – and gave me some of her young nephews' shirts saying they would fit me perfectly until I regained my normal weight. She is such a kindly soul and it relieves me greatly to know that she and Rosie are there at your side to nurse you back to health.

I was naturally also glad to have the chance to tell you about all the peculiar events that had begotten my ragged condition and I was doubly delighted by the fact that you appeared to believe me for, father, it pains me to say that when I returned to England my first port of call was to Mr Julius Colebridge at Piccadilly to relate my tale – and to justify in some manner the money he had kindly advanced with a view to publishing my joint volume with that scoundrel Mr Eustace Skate – but I was

horrified to discover how unconvinced he was as to the verac-
ity of my account and my fury at his implication that I was a
fantasist and a liar was such that I am ashamed to admit that
I thumped my fist down hard onto the table upsetting his cup
which rattled and tumbled spilling tea all over some import-
ant-looking papers! Assuring me that everything was fine as he
rang the little bell and watched his mouse-like secretary mop
up the offending liquid and I apologized profusely although
Mr Colebridge – gentleman that he is at his core – dismissed
it and, after the secretary had gone and I had calmed down a
little, he offered me a brandy and told me he had a proposition.
Naturally it is the one in which I am currently employed.

Father, when you asked me about how I was progressing in
London I must admit to a certain degree of fraudulence and
I wish to beg your forgiveness in this matter for I am not, as
I stated, working diligently on the account of my travels but,
rather, on something considerably less edifying. You see father,
Mr Colebridge believes in the power of the emerging popular
weekly journal and, as he soaked up the last of the tea from his
desk with his handkerchief, he explained that he had founded
one of these organs himself called 'The Extraordinary London
Gazette'. As publisher, proprietor and general editor, he offered
to consider publishing my account at some future date but said
that, in the meantime, it might serve me well to establish myself
as a journalist first so that when the book eventually emerged my
name would already be familiar to the reading public and that an
audience had therefore been secured for it. I was disappointed
by this development and, if truth be told, somewhat suspicious
of Mr Colebridge's strategy, but, father, since my return I am in
a state of comparative penury and my lodgings here in Islington
are hardly imposing – or, indeed, comfortable – so I had little
choice but to accept his offer for a small salary in the even-
tual hope of his promise about the book being honoured. In the
meantime he has teamed me up as a journalist on the 'Gazette'

with a rather taciturn but talented sketch-artist called Mr Bunch and our given task is to uncover and relate some of the more lurid and disconcerting and sensationalist events of the great city to a population which – as Mr Colebridge assured me – is becoming increasingly literate and hungry for titillation! I can only imagine your shame at this news dear father and I can only beg your forgiveness for lacking the courage to inform you of my situation in person last week at Havemore. But trust me that I will serve my apprenticeship with honour and diligence and, in time, my book will appear and I shall swell your noble heart with pride. I am grateful for the small parcel you arranged for me – Mrs Bartlett's lemon drizzle cake survived the journey remarkably well and had almost retained the full integrity of its original shape – but pray do not send more money. I am determined to make my own way in the city and to stand or fall by my own efforts. Mr Colebridge has called me in for a meeting in his office tomorrow morning so I am hopeful that he has finally agreed to my most recent letter whereupon I once again pleaded for his consideration regarding the commissioning of my book. I have spent the money you sent me on a new shirt and some shoes. I considered a hat but decided instead to keep the one I have. I shall write soon father. Please extend my gratitude to Mrs Bartlett for the cake.

Your loving son,
Hilary.

4. Being an account of a meeting with Mr Julius Colebridge Esq.

THROUGH THE OPEN window in Mr Colebridge's office I heard the incessant rattle of the coaches as they made their way down towards the Haymarket. The mesh of several hundred human voices coalesced into one cacophonous and unintelligible clamour.

"Is it too cold for you Hilary?" asked Mr Colebridge, pouring out some of the tea his secretary had just brought in on a tray. "I could always close the window."

"No sir. It's fine."

"Good," said Mr Colebridge, stirring his tea and moving over to the window to take in the air. "I like to hear and smell the city. Don't you?"

He half-turned.

"Yes sir."

I could smell horse dung and rotting fish from the streets below.

"Finest city in the world. I can't claim to be a well-travelled man but I have visited both Venice and Paris and although I can vouch for their magnificence I have to say that they can't match the wonders of London. Wouldn't you agree Hilary? What was it Dr Johnson said? Tired of London, tired of life? Very true I'd say. Very true."

Mr Colebridge took a deep breath. He sat behind his desk, carefully placed his cup of tea in front of him, picked up a piece of paper, adjusted his pince-nez to inspect it briefly, grunted as if it was unimportant and leant forward.

"How are you getting on?"

"Sir?"

"With Mr Bunch."

"He is a most... refreshing individual."

"Entirely self-taught you know. His father was a drunkard and his poor mother died when he was but a child. But he persevered at his craft and now I consider myself lucky to have secured his services at the *Gazette*."

Mr Colebridge stared at me like a lion carefully observing his prey.

"London must feel strange to you now Hilary, after such a long period away."

"I do consider myself to be something of a stranger at times, sir."

Mr Colebridge smiled.

"When you first told me the tale of your most astounding and singular adventures I must admit that I was somewhat amused, but nevertheless delighted by such a magnificent example of imaginative storytelling. The kite, the American gentleman – what was his name again? *Burgin?*"

"Burgess."

"Silver-haired warriors, shipwrecks, porcupines and all the rest of it."

He smiled again and shook his head.

"It is the very stuff of a first-class adventure novel and I wanted to let you know, Hilary, that I have had a quiet word with Jonathan Baxter over at Chapman and Hall and they are very interested in reading the synopsis with a view to considering the full text for publication next Spring. Now, what do you say to that my boy? Naturally you will have to amend the less than approbative remarks regarding Mr Eustace Skate and delete entirely the imaginary encounter with Sir Duncan Roseberry lest it be met with a charge of libel."

I placed my quivering cup and saucer on the table.

"Sir, I wouldn't want you for a minute to think that I was ungrateful for what you have done for me over the years. You were a good friend to my father at Cambridge and you have been supportive of him too and, indeed, upon my recent visit to Havemore Hall he told me that you had been kind enough to write to him regularly during his illness."

"He is recovering I hope?"

"Slowly sir. Yes."

"Good. Good."

Mr Colebridge created a triangle with his two index fingers and slowly placed his chin on the apex. I understood this to be an invitation to continue.

"I am, as I say, most appreciative of your efforts on my behalf sir, but I should once again like to stress that what happened was not a work of fiction or a trick of my imagination sir. My manuscript relates nothing but fact. Even the encounter with Sir Duncan."

The smile vanished from Mr Colebridge's face and he sat back in his chair with a sigh.

"Hilary, Hilary. Please."

He regarded me briefly with an expression of paternal sufferance before shaking his head.

"Your eloquence and imagination is something I've always admired. Your father's letter of introduction following your graduation informed me that you were intent on following the footsteps of the great explorers of our times and I was only pleased to help in whatever way I could. I teamed you up with Mr Skate with a view to producing a joint volume of travels which I felt could help in establishing you as a young writer of –"

The blood rushed to my head.

"I have to tell you Mr Colebridge, as I pointed out in my letter to you, that Mr Skate is nothing more than a *scoundrel* and –"

"Hilary, allow me to finish please."

My poor heart was a prisoner in my chest and it thumped the bars demanding its freedom but my mouth was frozen. I slumped back in my chair and would have picked up the teacup but I decided against it because I deduced, correctly, that my hands were still shaking with so much fury that the porcelain would have rattled and the, by now lukewarm, liquid would have most likely spilled out onto the Persian rug.

Mr Colebridge continued, his voice lower now and as calm and as steady as the Thames.

"I was more than happy to give you the opportunity to produce a volume of travel accounts Hilary but I was also aware, as you will appreciate, that you were relatively inexperienced as an author and so I decided that the best course would be to suggest Mr Eustace Skate – a most distinguished and famous explorer with a fine prose style – as a mentor and guide in a co-written book. Sadly, Mr Skate communicated to me that you absconded mysteriously one night in Singapore and that he never saw you again. He assured me with great sadness that he waited for you for a full morning by the quayside but that you never appeared and that –"

My fury got the better of me again.

"But that is not *true* sir! That is quite the *opposite* of what –"

"And *as a result*, he explained in his letter that under the circumstances he was forced to continue his journey alone and to abandon the joint volume in favour of his main passion, the search for the fabled monastery at Pan Reng. I naturally conceded to his request and agreed to forward him a modest amount of money towards his travel costs recoupable upon publication of his new book."

"You did not get my letter then sir?"

"*Letter?*"

"I wrote to you from the island. When I was rescued by the fishermen. Following the incident with the giant centipede. And the storm. Of course I didn't know the fishermen were evil then. But I escaped and then fought a porcupine. I placed it in a bottle. Along with one to my father."

There was a pause and I slowly recognized the expression on Mr Colebridge's face as one of muted alarm.

"No bottle was delivered."

Muted coaches rattled from the streets below. Birds twittered. Behind me, in the main office, the voices of clerks muttered and rumbled. My throat was dry but I didn't dare lift the teacup.

"It may yet arrive one day and be fished out of the Thames. I am *not* mad sir."

Mr Colebridge smiled like a sympathetic housemaster in response to a minor misdemeanour. Encouraged by this, I sat forward.

"I am sure, sir, that the truthfulness of my account would become apparent if you were ever to confront Sir Duncan Roseberry with it."

"Oh, I *did*."

"You *did*?"

"Yes. Last night at the Athenaeum. Obviously the sudden arrival back in London of a man of Sir Duncan's fame and popularity created surprise as well as excitement – or at least what passes for excitement within the dignified walls of the Athenaeum! I was lucky enough to have a short conversation with him over a brandy and, in the course of this conversation, I mentioned your name. But he didn't appear to recall it."

"He never could."

"When I told him of your account of what happened he laughed so uproariously that several members turned around to see what had generated such a powerful response. He assured me that his account of his discovery of the Tower at Ectha was the true one and that he would prove it his forthcoming public lecture at Haberdashers Hall by means of his sketches and journals. The tower, he said, was virtually intact and almost a thousand feet high. Perhaps you should attend the talk Hilary? Eustace Skate will also be present to talk of his discovery of the monastery at Pan Reng."

My heart raced at the thought of both men being in London once again and, worse, being celebrated for their crimes.

Fury once more overcame me.

"Sir Duncan Roseberry is a *fraud* and a *trickster*! And Mr Skate a *duplicitous rogue!*"

Mr Colebridge regarded me with an expression of shock, then disappointment. He took a deep breath which signified that he had something uncomfortable to communicate.

"Hilary," he said, clearly trying to keep his tone as measured as he could. "I have been involved with travellers and gentlemen explorers for many years and one thing that has struck me is the fact that the many strange and astonishing sights and sounds they witness sometimes can have a distinct – and not always beneficial – effect on their judgement."

"I am not mad."

"Pray let me finish."

Mr Colebridge took a deep breath which signified that he had something uncomfortable to communicate.

"Hilary, the morning you left my office after agreeing the contract with myself and Mr Eustace Skate can only have happened two or three years ago and yet, looking at you now, any neutral observer who happened to venture upon this little scene would surely surmise that you had been away for *fifty*! I am not accustomed to judging a man by his appearance Hilary but, well…"

Mr Colebridge coughed discreetly and adjusted a pen on his table for no other reason than to cover his embarrassment.

"I couldn't help but notice your teeth – or the lack of them. And you are so very *thin* boy. What you need is a sizzling pork chop from Mr Earnest's! What on earth do you sustain yourself with?"

"This and that sir."

"Hilary, as an old friend of your father's I feel a certain obligation to his only son. That is why I was more than happy to invite you to be involved in my exciting new venture."

He beamed, clapped his hands, stood up, went over to the window and took in a generous lungful of the odious Piccadilly air.

"There's a whole new world out there Hilary! A world of opportunities for men with vision and ideas. *Literacy*! It's a most wonderful gift and now, thanks to our advances in education, we have an enormous amount of literate and modestly prosperous people out there desperate for something to transport them out of the dullness of their everyday drudgery. Why, even the neediest of the London poor are now able to at least read a page of an average newspaper if it's presented to them simply and clearly."

He came back to the desk, sat down heavily and lowered his voice. It trembled with excitement.

"Murder, rape, burglary, kidnapping! That is what this new readership wants and craves and, by God sir, that is what I aim to give them in the pages of *The Extraordinary London Gazette!*"

He sat forward; his eyes shining with zeal.

"Work with me Hilary. Hone your skills. Bring yourself back to full health and gain a reputation. Be there when they catch this infernal monster The Slasher and write up the full story in the pages of the *Gazette*! Let's beat that horde of other journalists who are on his trail. Then, perhaps, we can think of books. What do you say?"

As Mr Colebridge smiled eagerly at me from across the desk a small, grey sparrow landed on the sill of the open window. After a melodious trill, he fluttered into the room and landed on my shoulder, pecking my ear gently and affectionately before allowing himself to be cupped in my hand. I stroked the top of his head with my finger before the bird unleashed another melody, purred back to the sill, picked at his feathers with his beak and vanished into the London sky.

Mr Colebridge frowned curiously. He looked at me. Then at the window. Then back at me.

"How *remarkable!*"

5. I am briefly – and anonymously – re-acquainted with my nemesis.

FROM ACROSS THE Mall I observed the lighted rooms of the Athenaeum Club. I saw the various gentlemen cross the windows occasionally, some deep in conversation, others laughing. Another window on a different level offered a tantalizing glimpse of a wall of leather-bound books and I briefly imagined myself sitting in this library sipping a brandy whilst flicking the pages of one of these venerable tomes and puffing at a pipe.

"Here, watch where you're going!"

A young gentleman in a top hat prodded me painfully in the shoulder with his cane and I stood back to allow him to pass. He frowned at me but then continued on his way. When I looked up at the library window again I saw a servant of the club drawing the curtains to block out the world.

Pulling up the collar of my coat up against the cold evening air I watched the coaches rattling by. They criss-crossed themselves expertly as they carried their passengers across the great city, the varnished black and gold of the carriages glinting as they caught the streetlights and the arrogant clopping horses as heroic as any from the pages of Homer. Whenever one of the carriages stopped outside the doors of the Athenaeum I straightened myself and peered through the annoying mesh of traffic to see if it contained either Sir Duncan Roseberry or Eustace Skate but having stood on the pavement for over an hour and a half, neither of them had stepped out and walked up the steps of the club to be greeted by the doffed hat of the doorman.

This doorman had observed me with suspicion for a while and had, on one occasion, pointed me out to a colleague but I presumed they were bound by the perimeters of the doorway and had no authority outside their little kingdom to remove me or shoo me away. The doorman had waved angrily at me but I'd ignored him. By now, as another coach pulled up to the club, he had obviously concluded that I was simply a harmless beggar and had decided to ignore me too. The coach unloaded a portly man who struggled up the few stairs to the front doors of the club. The doorman tried to help him but he was furiously waved away and I allowed myself a smile of satisfaction.

The air was getting colder and the condensation from my breath formed thick clouds around my head. The torn and dusty coat offered scant protection. Had Mr Colebridge been mistaken? Were Sir Duncan Roseberry and Mr Eustace Skate genuinely frequenting the Athenaeum since their return? Could it have been another establishment? The Travellers Club perhaps? I was on the verge of giving up my attempt to catch a glimpse of my two enemies when I heard a familiar voice approaching along the pavement. I turned and saw Sir Duncan Roseberry and another gentleman walking towards me. Sir Duncan was accompanied by a beautiful young lady in a blue coat. Her golden ringlets tumbled exquisitely around her face, bouncing as she walked along and her feet – encased in delicate black shoes – were as small as a child's. Whenever she laughed – and it was often because whatever Sir Duncan seemed to be saying was proving to be of the utmost amusement to her – it sounded as delightful as a perfectly executed arpeggio on an angel's harp. Transfixed and somewhat mesmerised by the beauty of the young lady in the blue coat I forgot to move aside as they came closer.

"Out of the way," snarled Sir Duncan, clearly annoyed that his highly amusing story to the young lady had been interrupted and waving his cane like a sword in my direction. "Damned impertinence!"

Glancing at me, the beautiful young lady's smile froze and slowly mutated into an expression of distaste. I felt a peculiar pang of guilt at having been responsible for halting her enjoyment, however briefly. But I also noticed that she was not as young as I'd previously imagined. Judging by the amount of powder on her cheeks I calculated that she was perhaps thirty. In her prime I imagined that her beauty would have been even more potent and was of the kind that could have been as cruel as a blade to any man who was unfortunate enough to be spurned. I took off my hat deferentially and attempted to control my unruly hair but the lady was not impressed.

"He smells."

She waved one of her gloved hands in front of her face and crinkled up her nose.

"You are right my dear," said Sir Duncan, winking at her mischievously and causing her smile to return like sunlight from behind a cloud. "I wonder what it might be."

He came closer and made a big show of breathing in the air.

"*Garlic* I'd say. With a hint of haddock. And three or four days of accumulated sweat of course. What say you Skate?"

Skate?

I studied Sir Duncan Roseberry's companion closer and saw that, indeed, he was my former nemesis! Heavier and now possessed of a mighty beard, I had not recognized him immediately.

"I'd rather not venture any closer if you don't mind Sir Duncan."

"No," said Sir Duncan thoughtfully. "It is probably for the best."

I noticed the scimitar birthmark on Sir Duncan's forehead. Since I last saw him – at a time which seemed to me to be a thousand years ago – his skin had regained its former lustre and his hair was as thick as hay.

"Do you gentlemen not recognise me?" I said.

"Speak up man! What did you say?"

My words had been obscured by a passing coach. I opened my mouth to speak again but I was interrupted by Eustace Skate.

"Here," he said, tossing me a penny. "Get yourself a bath. Come Sir Duncan. We'll be late."

"Indeed," said Sir Duncan Roseberry, hooking his arm around the lady by his side and causing her to giggle in a rather exaggerated and ungainly fashion, "let us go Penelope my dear."

As they walked away, among the laughter from the lady and Sir Duncan, I heard Eustace Skate uttering that the streets of London were a menace these days and that something should be done. Sir Duncan Roseberry gladly concurred and his Penelope giggled.

6. A melancholy reflection and the threat of violence.

MY MODEST LODGING in Islington felt as distant as India and my feet were aching. I had walked for miles along the London streets powered only by a desire for my warm bed and a thirst for revenge. But what could a man in my position do? Protected by fame and the trappings of wealth and status men like Sir Duncan Roseberry and Eustace Skate were invincible. I reasoned that tonight had probably been the closest I would ever come to initiating any kind of righteous vengeance but I too had been momentarily mesmerized by their presence just as the giggling Penelope had been. Entranced and bewitched, my body had become as limp as a blade of grass waving in the breeze. Now, as I passed the raucous taverns and gin houses, I clenched my fists and realized that I should have struck them both to the ground and kicked them as hard as I could but bravery and purpose in retrospect was as fine – and ultimately as useless – as a porcelain vase. But it had probably been for the best. Sir Duncan Roseberry's famous pugilistic skills would have saved him from any serious damage from a depleted and ragged specimen such as myself whilst Eustace Skate would have doubtlessly stepped in and pummelled me mercilessly with his cane. With my feet dragging along the pavement and my head bowed I arrived at the inevitable – and it must be conceded – astoundingly unoriginal conclusion that the world was not fair and that the evil, deceptive actions of unscrupulous individuals were not always punished. Looking up at the night sky and at the stars which glinted coldly out of the blackness I wondered if there was, in fact, a benevolent God, framed, naturally, in the shape of a fair-minded English gentleman, looking down upon his creation and ensuring that a fundamental sense of justice would always prevail, or if the sky merely stretched away into chaos and anarchy – a smattering of whirling rocks and stones untroubled by morality, ethics or law. Despondent and disillusioned, I stepped into a tavern, took out the penny Eustace Skate had tossed at me and bought a tankard of ale. Avoiding a raucous crew of labourers who were singing and laughing in the centre of the room – nudging me as I passed and inviting me to join in whatever mysterious celebration they were enjoying – I sat down in a dark corner and supped my bitter nectar.

How had the two explorers not recognized me?

The question circled in my mind like an albatross. Surely any man who had betrayed a colleague in such a bare-faced manner as Eustace Skate had done in Singapore would always be haunted by the face of his victim and by a strong sense of shame and guilt? Similarly, Sir Duncan Roseberry – having executed the most blatant and ruthless trick on a naïve and slightly overawed young man such as me – would also have his sorry face imprinted upon his brain forever? But evidently not. As I supped the ale again and glanced across at the dancing labourers I concluded that men like Sir Duncan Roseberry and Eustace Skate owed a great part of their fame and success to a certain sense of isolation from the world around them. I smiled to myself as I considered the ironic fact that these two gentlemen were lauded and honoured for their services to shedding light on previously unknown sections of the world whilst they were also, curiously, staggeringly blind to it. As they travelled they saw the wonders of the globe only in relation to themselves and their glory. Each mysterious cave became another book. An oriental monastery a possible knighthood. Men like that would never remember an unimportant figure such as myself. I had been less than a footnote in ether of their stories – as unworthy of their attention as any of the cobblestones or slats I had walked on since our meeting that night.

I supped again. Wiped my mouth with my sleeve and slapped the tankard down on the table. I realized too, of course, that there were other factors which had contributed to their lack of recognition. My clothes were far from being the finest – in fact they were worn and thin – whilst my hair felt as dry straw. Long and unruly, it stuck out in all manner of different directions and would have been greatly served by the attentions of a competent barber if only I had the means to afford one. In the mornings I would douse it with water and comb it back in an attempt to give it at least some semblance of order but, by the end of the day, it had once again staged a revolt and exploded into a riot. No wonder neither gentleman had recognized me. Even my poor father had struggled to see his son in the tangled mess who had stood before him on my return to Havemore Hall and Mrs Bartlett, at first, had screamed and picked up a broom for her immediate defence.

I finished the ale, sat back in my chair and pushed away the tankard. As I glanced at all the faces in the room – some singing and laughing, others arguing and pointing – I wondered how many of these faces I myself would remember in five or maybe ten minutes. And, with a painful pang of realization, I understood that I too had been infected by the single-minded selfishness of Sir Duncan Roseberry and Eustace Skate for had I myself not condemned a poor and innocent young man to a terrible fate back on that island? Poor Tobias Gently. I imagined him standing there, crucified against the rocks of the ancient tower on the other side of the world, his clothes rags and his body skin and bone. Dying whilst dreaming of his faithless and undeserving Penelope. Did the birds come and feed him like they'd fed Sir Duncan and myself or had he and the tower long since collapsed into the sand to be forever forgotten?

But Tobias Gently was *not* forgotten. For as I looked at all the faces in the tavern I realized that if the poor young fellow walked into the room at that very moment – thin as a stick and with his once innocent face disfigured by hate and the desire for revenge – I would have recognized him immediately as his eyes sought out, almost by instinct, the dishevelled and sad form of the man in the dark corner with his empty tankard. My heart would have jumped up almost as quickly as my body. I would have walked up to him, fallen to my knees and, in tears, tugged at his rags and begged his forgiveness. The dancing labourers and the arguing men in the far corner would have been silenced by such a strange action and Tobias Gently would have stared down at me, his eyes now hardened by months trapped at sea on a Portuguese clipper which had happened by and rescued him. Would he have wanted to kill me for perpetuating this cycle of cruelty and self-preservation? Had he too been forced to issue his escape only by tricking another curious and innocent soul at the Tower of Ectha? In my panic I looked around the room once again, the sweat forming on my forehead and on my palms. Now, instead of the red-faced labourers and the warty arguers I only saw the face of Tobias Gently on everyone there – young, unlined and smiling, just as it had that day when I'd first encountered him at the tower. The landlord had his face. As did the labourer who had nudged me and invited me to dance. They were both smiling at me – pointing and laughing. *Two Tobias Gentlys!* With four more behind them! *A tavern full of Tobias Gentlys!* Their voices blending into his. The faces and voices of Tobias Gently tormenting me and reminding me of my guilt. My selfishness. The fact that I too had been a trickster and a fraud unworthy of redemption and likely to be admonished and cleansed only by forgiveness!

I stood up and approached the dancing labourer, grabbing his hand.

"Forgive me," I said.

"'Ere, what are you doing?"

The labourer shook me off and, in an instant, the face of Tobias Gently was replaced by the labourer's angry scowl.

"I'm sorry," I said. "Forgive me. I..."

I loosened my grip on the labourer's hand and he pushed me away. Once exposed in the middle of the room – which had been mysteriously and suddenly cleared as all the other customers formed a makeshift ring to witness the consequences with evident pleasure, clapping their hands and leering – I fully expected to be pummelled into a pulp by the labourer's fists which were clenching and unclenching rhythmically at the end of his tree-trunk arms. But, after a few seconds of gritting his teeth and muttering threats under his breath he clearly decided that I was an unworthy opponent and he half turned away, waving me off like a fly and returning to his ale. The other patrons looked at each other with disappointment and they assumed their previous positions and conversations.

I left the tavern and walked up the street at twice my original pace keeping my head down and avoiding looking into strangers' faces lest I should again be tricked by the illusion of seeing Tobias Gently at every corner. Sweating profusely and now, due to the ale – which had been stronger than I'd expected – and by my speed, somewhat unsteady on my feet, I could at least console myself that, unlike Sir Duncan Roseberry and Eustace Skate I did not forget the faces of the ones I had tricked. I remembered my past misdemeanours with a tremendous wave of guilt and was fully prepared to make amends.

7. The loneliness of Islington proves to be deceptive.

AS THE STREETS quietened I became aware of the sound of my own footsteps on the pavement. By now I calculated that I must have been walking for almost an hour since leaving the tavern and therefore almost two hours since my meeting with Sir Duncan Roseberry and Eustace Skate. My poor feet were sore and I hoped that the thin, worn leather of my shoes would withstand the remainder of my journey to my lodgings. Once home I would boil the kettle on the fire, prepare a soothing cup of tea and try to forget the feelings of hate that had been rekindled outside the Athenaeum and the peculiar illusion that had haunted me inside the tavern. All would be well in the morning, I told myself, increasing my pace slightly. *All will be well in the morning.* An invisible owl hooted from a nearby tree and emphasised the relative silence of Islington for, in the previous ten minutes or so, only one carriage had clattered past. The driver had raised his hat and the coach had been empty. Now, as the owl's cry was absorbed by the blackness, the only sounds were the occasional rush of a breeze and the scraping of a dismembered newspaper as it was bullied across the cobblestones. Fragments of muffled conversations escaped through the lower gaps of doors and open windows of houses and as I stopped and turned briefly I saw the glow of distant London against the night sky. Somewhere in that shimmering dome Sir Duncan Roseberry and Eustace Skate were laughing and drinking as they entertained each other – and doubtlessly tried to outdo each other – with tales of derring do in exotic climes whilst an appreciative audience encouraged them, hanging on every word and applauding. Somewhere too the Prime Minister was probably scrutinizing some important piece of legislature – spectacles firmly attached as he stifled a yawn and considered the haven of his bed – for even Prime Ministers were obliged to sleep. Mr Julius Colebridge was probably snoring and dreaming of the money he would make from the *Gazette* whilst, in the maze-like lanes of Whitechapel or the Seven Dials, The Slasher was prowling the streets like a wolf, his knife glinting in the moonlight – his next victim smiling innocently at him from a doorway, unaware that he or she would shortly be ripped apart and reduced to a filthy pile of offal.

I continued walking and was only a few streets away from my lodging when I became aware of the feeling that I was being followed. I stopped and turned around but all I could see was an empty street. The outskirts were less well-served by gas lights but their dim shimmering revealed nothing other than some distressed leaves conspiring secretly in rustling circles. I raised my collar against the cold and continued walking but after only a few yards I was once again struck by this eerie conviction that I was not alone and so, with my heart beating so hard that I could almost hear it, I stopped for a second time and peered into the darkness. The gas light was now further away and the shadows were thick and as impenetrable as granite but the presence of someone else in the shadows was confirmed when a gang of rats scuttled away for safety across the road.

"Hello," I said, the tremor clearly audible in my voice. "Is there anyone there?"

Nothing but the breeze and the whispering leaves. In the distance there was the rattle of a carriage and a couple of barking dogs.

"I have no money," I said into the darkness, desperately attempting to conceal my nervousness. "If you mean to rob me you will only find the rags I am wearing."

I took a tentative step forward in case my invisible tracker was observing me – which I was sure that he was – and wished to convey the sense that I was not scared. Which, of course, I *was*.

After a few seconds more of nothing but the barking dogs and the nervous leaves I turned on my heels and walked on, increasing my pace but hoping that whoever it was that was following me would not notice. Then, just before the end of the street, I turned swiftly into a dark alley and pushed myself as hard as I could against the wall adopting the same crucified pose that I had at the hard stones of the Tower of Ectha. Hardly daring to breathe I turned my head to the direction of the street and waited to see who it was that was so intent on pursuing me. When nothing or no one came I began to wonder if I'd imagined the entire thing. The ale in the tavern had – as I previously indicated – been strong and it had led to me believing that the whole room was full of Tobias Gentlys so why would I now not be fooled into thinking that some petty street thief had mistaken me for a rich gentleman and was now determined to assault me? Feeling slightly idiotic and thankful that no one else had been around to witness my folly I relaxed my crucified pose. I glanced out to the street and a devilish black shape came into view momentarily before slinking by. It was silent and graceful.

And possessed a long, swishing tail.

8. Mr Harry Bunch considers the probable characteristics of The Slasher.

"*RUDRA*," SAID HARRY Bunch, pushing down the tobacco in his briar pipe. "It means the 'remover of pain' so they say. And how right they are. Because I tell you, if anything was more likely to rid you of all worldly woes then it would be a fierce black panther from the depths of the Indian jungle!"

He issued a raspy laugh, clearly pleased with his observation.

"But how did he escape? Surely the walls of the Zoological Gardens are intended to be impassable."

The wrinkles of laughter on Harry Bunch's face smoothed out slowly. He placed his unlit pipe down on the table.

"You must have witnessed the behaviour of wild beasts?"

"A few."

"Well then you'll know how cunning they can be."

Harry Bunch leant forward, placed both elbows on the table and glanced quickly over his shoulders as if the entire establishment was full of informers and spies.

"The way I heard it," he said, lowering his voice. "His keeper – a faithful chap who'd been with him since he arrived here a few months ago from Madras – turned his back on the animal as he cleaned out his cage but those few seconds were enough. The deplorable cat attacked this poor fellow and would have probably torn him to shreds had not the lure of the open door been more attractive. Not the first time it's happened apparently. Rudra sneaked out last week too but was recaptured in Stepney. Took three men to hold him down and one of them lost a hand. Detestable things panthers."

Harry Bunch picked up the pipe, shoved the tobacco even further down into the bowl with his thumb.

"The keeper probably owes his life to that open door."

My colleague lit the pipe and acrid tobacco billowed into the room. The smoke was almost too much for him for he coughed a few times even though he tried to hide it.

"I think I *saw* him. Rudra."

Harry Bunch looked up.

"Last night," I said. "I was returning from the Athe–" I stopped myself in case I was asked any awkward questions about my reasons for having loitered outside that noble establishment. "As I was returning *from town*. I was approaching my lodgings and..."

I took a deep breath and met Harry Bunch's gaze with an intensity which clearly impressed upon him that this was no joke. I lowered my voice just like he had done.

"I *heard* him first," I said. "I naturally thought maybe it was a street robber so I walked a little faster. I took advantage of a dark alley and lurked in the shadows to let him pass. But after a few seconds I saw a long black shape with a tail. I must admit that I doubted my own eyes. I waited for what must have been a full ten minutes before I even dared to move again. Eventually I hurried back to my lodgings, fumbling all the while in my pockets for the keys! I was sure that I had experienced another peculiar vision. I am troubled by them quite regularly."

"How bizarre."

"I realize now of course that I was not being pursued by one of Satan's angels but was, in all probability, being trailed by an escaped panther with a view to furnishing him with a convenient supper! Have they recaptured him?"

Harry Bunch shook his head gravely.

"People say cats ain't as clever as dogs but I disagree. Give a cat an inch and he'll snatch a yard just as soon as look at you. And these streets and alleyways are like a home from home to a panther. London's a jungle of a different kind Hilary. I reckon it could take a while for them to get him this time. He's cunning.

But he's also black. And he only comes out at night. You get my drift I'm guessing."

"Indeed I do Mr Bunch. Indeed I do."

A clock chimed at the far corner of the tavern. Harry Bunch took out his pocket watch, held it up to his ear and shook it.

"Damn thing! It's stopped again. And I only took it in to Mr Shellcock's in Holborn last week. I'll have to take it in again."

He slipped it back in his pocket and tapped out his pipe on the edge of the table.

"Come on, drink up. We're late."

9. One butcher evaluates the handiwork of another.

THE BODY THIS time was that of a young man. I surmised that he may have been a clerk for there were some papers still slightly glued to his glistening flesh. They flapped gently in the breeze – whatever importance they may have had now rendered completely irrelevant.

"Poor chap," said the butcher, wiping his hands on his apron and taking a whistling intake of breath through his pursed lips. "Know him did you?"

"No," said Harry Bunch and myself in unison.

The butcher nodded. If he thought our interest in the body was strange he didn't verbalize it. He glanced down at the corpse again.

"I came out back this morning soon as I got in – must have been about four – I was slopping out the worktop, emptying everything into that barrel over there just like normal – when I saw him lying there and that was definitely *not* normal. I can assure you of that gentlemen. I've seen some pretty ripe sights in my life. I used to work in the gut-scraping sheds at Harrow Alley. But nothing there could match what happened to this poor bastard. 'Ere, let me move that chair for you."

"It's quite alright," said Harry Bunch, scribbling in his sketch book.

"Whatever it was he was running from must have been pretty damn scary. Only fear could get a man over my back wall. Six foot high it is. Not that it did him any good. Whatever was after him got over it too."

The butcher turned to me and wiped his hands on his grey, blood-soaked apron.

"Sam Coulder," he said proudly. "Purveyor of fine meats and poultry. Game too when I can get it."

He shook my hand and I felt his fingers dig into my palm almost as if he was assessing the quality of my flesh.

"I'll let you gentlemen get on. Anything you need, just give me a shout. I'll only be in that side room cutting up a pig."

Once Mr Coulder was inside I stepped over a mattress and approached Harry Bunch.

"I have a theory."

He glanced sideways at me but didn't stop sketching. I cleared my throat and tried not to look at the mangled corpse which was now wearing a buzzing shroud of black flies.

"What if all the authorities and the Peelers have got it all wrong? What if there isn't a dangerous and vengeful man with a knife and a hateful heart prowling the streets of our city? What if, instead, there's a large Indian panther with a hunger for human flesh? You can see for yourself Mr Bunch that parts of this unfortunate fellow have been ripped out and have disappeared. Perhaps Rudra ate them?"

Harry Bunch continued sketching. A wry smile formed on his face.

"It had occurred to me too," he said.

"Oh. Really?"

I was vaguely disappointed at my clear lack of originality. Harry Bunch turned to me, tucking his sketchbook in his inside pocket.

"But the flaw in the theory is this. Rudra only escaped the other night. The Slasher has now claimed seven victims – *eight* if you include this unfortunate chap. For your theory to hold water then Rudra would have had to escape from his cage at the Zoological Gardens every night for the last couple of months, commit terrible acts of murder on seemingly random individuals on the streets of London, return to his cage, remove all traces of blood and entrails from his jowls and then, finally, lock himself back in."

He placed his arm on my shoulder. Of course he was correct.

"So what kind of demon could *do* this?" I whispered.

10. A further letter home.

Holborn, July 20th

My dear father,

It was good to receive the parcel today – it was waiting for me as I returned from the courts and delivered safely into my hands by Mrs Northcote who emerged from her rooms and hailed me as I walked up the stairs to my attic apartment. How wonderfully packed it was! Surely it cannot have been your handiwork father? I remember fondly how you struggled with even the most basic elements of practicability and often had to rely on Old Jacob to come to your aid whenever you were faced with such insurmountable problems such as a loose door handle, creaking floorboard or, once, that memorable instance when you hurled a new boot to the far side of the drawing room when the challenge of lacing it up proved to be as laborious and exhausting as the one which faced poor Sisyphus! So I imagine Mrs Bartlett must have assumed the responsibility of creating such a tight and delightful bundle – or perhaps the new man, what is his name again? Hewlett? – might have helped? It is of no consequence. The flat cakes were a delight (inform Mrs Bartlett that I scoffed them all in one sitting with my tea!).

Father, I was glad to hear from you also how Doctor Bell-weather's attentions appeared to have had such dramatic beneficial results. His suggestion that you visit Waltzburg for a few weeks clearly proved to be inspired for the ingestion the famous waters must have rejuvenated both your flesh and spirits. However, despite this I must ask you to reconsider your expressed intention to visit me here in London, at least for the time being, for – delightful as it would be to see you father – I fear that the relentless bustle of this city would be most dele-terious to your progress at this moment. By all means come to London but I beg you to postpone until the Spring.

You will of course have seen from the top of this letter that I have moved lodging since I last wrote. I received word from Mr Bunch a month or so ago that these rooms in Holborn were suddenly free and being more central, would be most conve-nient. They are larger too. Now I have a modest lounge in addition to even more modest sleeping quarters together with a sizeable fireplace which, unlike the last place, is large enough to boil a kettle. My landlady is a certain Mrs Northcote. She hails originally from Faversham and, despite her somewhat brusque manner at the early stages of our arrangement, she had since become rather more amenable and only yesterday – upon my return and as I was creeping up the creaking stairs in an attempt to go unheeded – she emerged from her rooms on the ground floor red-faced and animated with a plate of lard cakes which she had just taken out of the stove! I have to say father that they were most delicious.

You enquired about your old friend Mr Colebridge and he is as energetic and ambitious as ever! The 'Gazette' is proving to be a great success and the fortnightly editions are quickly becom-ing an essential accessory to London life it seems for, wherever I go on the day of publication – which is a Thursday – I see people queuing up at the street vendors to secure a copy. Then, as I walk around the streets of Piccadilly and Charing Cross, it would sometimes appear that every single Londoner is either carrying a rolled-up edition or is reading it on street corners, benches or chop houses. Why, only yesterday I happened to be crossing a busy Regent Street when I was almost run over by a carriage where the driver was actually reading a copy!

The only general concern at the 'Gazette' now – unspoken but nevertheless palpable – is whether the paper can sustain this level of ubiquity and popularity now that we have lost two of our major stories. You may have read in The Times father that the mass murderer whom we and the entire city dubbed 'The Slasher' has been caught red-handed – quite literally in his case – and, following a swift judgement at the Old Bailey, a certain Corville Swanston was convicted. Like all murderers he protested his innocence – quite vehemently in his case – saying that that the blood-soaked knife that was in his hand as he was apprehended by the Peelers was purely for self-defence for he had just been attacked by a giant cat which he insisted was out to slaughter him. However, when the prosecutor invited him to describe this mysterious animal Mr Swanston was quite definite in his description which, sadly for him, did not tally in any way with that of an escaped panther called Rudra which, in any event, had already been re-captured a few nights earlier outside the Palace of Westminster and so poor Mr Swanston's sole source of credible defence crumbled and his fate was sealed. The poor wretch hangs tomorrow afternoon at Newgate and a huge crowd is anticipated. Mr Bunch and myself will naturally be there in our official capacities. It will be my first ever public hanging father and I must admit to being a little uneasy but Mr Bunch assures me that it is all over in an instant and that it is not as gruesome as a beheading he witnessed in Bremen a few years ago. I am told that the funfair is the largest yet seen.

Father I must close now but rest assured that I will write again soon and please pass on my good wishes to Mrs Bartlett, Rosie and the new man. Do not exert yourself unnecessarily father, remember what the doctor said and take exercise in moderation.

Your loving son, Hilary.

11. A most distressing occurrence at Newgate.

"*WATCH IT MISTER!*"
The urchin who had collided with me was, by my rough calculation, around ten or eleven years old and was eager to catch up with his equally rambunctious friends. Without waiting to be admonished that perhaps it was *he*, rather than myself who should have been the vigilant party, he served me with a most disagreeable expression of disgust and weaved himself into the crowd. Gazing up at the blue, cloudless sky I could not escape the sense of incongruity that such a perfectly crisp late autumn day could be hosting such a lugubrious event as a public hanging. But, judging by the loud and excited behaviour of the hundreds – possibly even *thousands* – who had gathered on the green outside the prison walls to witness the execution of Corville Swanston – otherwise known as the infamous Slasher – I appeared to be alone in my sense of unease. Young women had dressed up in their finest silks and the wealthier among them sneered at the inferior efforts of their poorer cousins – some trying to cover their disdain by fanning their faces, others being more brazen and aloof. The gentlemen present seemed to ignore their social inferiors entirely, almost as if they did not even exist in the same world, let alone the same city. They gathered together with their top hats and canes, laughing raucously every now and then whilst looking around to see if there were any other members of their exclusive club present. All the while the poor milled around these islands of splendour like grey water – boys with dirty faces and ripped trousers; girls with skirts made out of bedding; cripples and beggars with rattling tin cups and well-practised expressions of woe; women

with missing teeth; men with ragged hair – and their voices melded into one cacophonous symphony of English discordant in accent, keys and emphasis. Away in the distance the freshly constructed gallows loomed amongst the merriment. A team of carpenters were hastily making some last-minute adjustments, their foreman gesticulating wildly whilst holding what appeared to be a mallet.

Harry Bunch nudged me.

"Let's get closer. They'll be bringing him out soon. I want to catch that look of fear."

I followed his lead as he pushed through the throng. As we got closer to the gallows the crowd became more dense and rather less genteel – some refused to budge at all and we were forced to work around them like a rivulet blocked by rocks. I quickly learned that manners were wasted in this situation and soon abandoned my apologies and hat-doffing. One woman elbowed me in the side and a young child kicked me in the shins but due largely to Harry Bunch's admirable intransigence and singular sense of purpose we soon found ourselves less than fifty yards away from the gallows in a small clearing which had been occupied by some traders and charlatans. One of the stalls was making brisk business in selling a wooden toy representing a miniature version of the gallows with a body dangling down from it on a piece of string. Some children were running around shrieking with delight as they watched the little wooden man dance and shake. They were selling for tuppence each and I could see that the seller had several of them at the back of his stall and that there was also a couple of men hastily constructing more. We passed a row of stands selling sizzling chops, frothing ale, sweets, hats, canes, coats and boots. There was even a vendor of our biggest rival – '*The Piccadilly Trumpet*' – holding up a hastily published edition of the paper emblazoned with the headline '*CORVILLE SWANSTON – MY CONFESSION*'. Knowing how contemptuously the editor of this scurrilous organ was held in the opinion of Mr Julius Colebridge I concluded that the alleged 'confession' was no doubt entirely fictitious but I also had to concede that – immoral hound that he was – he had struck a chord with his readership and possibly even enlarged it by his deception, for a large queue had formed in front of him and several ladies to my left were shrieking in horror as they read the alleged confession of The Slasher which, no doubt, some poor scribe had produced in the early hours of the morning before his work was rushed off to the printers. I glanced up at the gallows and my stomach turned as I saw the workmen pulling their ladders away, their tools already stuffed into their bags and belts. One of them stayed behind briefly to test one of the main poles by shaking it vigorously. Seemingly satisfied that it was sturdy enough for the job he walked away. The noose rocked slightly from left to right like a morbid pendulum. A couple of burly men shouted at the crowds down at the very front and I imagined that they were being admonished for pushing forward in order to get a better view. One of the men threw a bucket of water over them but, although there were screams and protests, this method had clearly been attempted several times to no avail.

"I doubt if we can get any closer than this," I said.

Harry Bunch shot me a look of disdain.

"Come on."

I was cursed with a creeping sense of unease but I also knew that my role was to report events and that my partner would no doubt view any reticence on my part as being not only deeply unprofessional but also disloyal. So I followed him as best I could as Harry Bunch pushed his way to the far side of the clearing towards where the crowds at the front had formed. We passed a small funfair with swings for the children and mysterious tents promising unusual spectacles for the adults. One moustachioed and bowler-hatted man had tucked his thumbs into his waistcoat and was proclaiming proudly that inside his little tent was a group of genuine savages from the depths of the jungle.

"Trust me ladies and gentlemen," he shouted, "you won't see anything like this ever again in your lives! The living Horrific Snow Monster from the mysterious heights of the Himalayas! Unschooled in the ways of Christian morality! Bound by chains! Here in the flesh and as real as yer breakfast!"

The crowd of men, women and children who had gathered around the little tent gasped and chattered excitedly.

"So come along then ladies and gentlemen," said the bowler-hatted man after checking his pocket-watch, "who will be the first to witness this rare sight? For your amazement and delight we also have the Dancing Chicken of Paris and the Eight-Legged Spider Woman of Singapore! All for only tuppence! Line up ladies and gentlemen, you won't be disappointed and this will be a sight that no one in the fair city of London will ever see again!"

But despite his finest persuasive efforts none of his audience appeared prepared to part with their money to witness such allegedly unique phenomenons. Sweating now, and with his face rapidly adopting the hue of a strawberry, he took off his bowler hat, wiped his balding head with his sleeve, fanned himself quickly with the rim and then donned it once more. Surreptitiously he took a step back and tugged at the flap of his little tent before stepping forwards again and smiling falsely as if nothing had happened – and, indeed, I was sure that I had been the only one there to notice it. A few seconds after this manoeuvre there were the clear signals of a violent commotion within the tent and some members of the gathered throng gasped.

"Don't worry ladies and gentlemen," said the sweaty, strawberry-faced man in the bowler hat – rather obviously feigning concern – "you are perfectly safe. The Horrific Snow Monster is securely tied up in chains and there is absolutely no chance of...*escape!*"

He emphasised the final word and half-turned back towards the tent and it was then that a white, furry creature dashed out with what appeared to be broken chains dangling from both his wrists. Stopping momentarily, he gazed hypnotically at the crowd and at his surroundings as if he had just awoken from a deep sleep. Then, roaring like a beast, he thumped his chest and unleashed a blood-curdling roar. Some of the ladies in the crowd screamed, holding on to their male companions for protection although, by my observation, even these guardians appeared to be apprehensive at the sudden manifestation of this strange apparition.

"Oh dear!" said the blower-hatted man somewhat unconvincingly, "the Horrific Snow Monster of the Himalayas appears to have broken free! Back!" he shouted, aiming his comments at the creature as if he was reprimanding a disobedient dog. *"Back I say!"*

But the creature just roared again and the ladies screamed.

"I do apologize ladies and gentlemen," said the bowler-hatted man, his nervousness somewhat contrived, "this has never happened before. Those chains are normally so strong and secure! *Back! Come back here!"*

Snarling, the furry beast ran towards me and we collided. I was pushed back a couple of feet by his momentum but regained my balance and stared into his face. The whiteness around his face morphed almost supernaturally into silver.

"You killed me," he said, quietly. "Back on the island. With your bayonet. I saved you. You gave me your good book. But then you gave me death. You too will die."

I saw the face of the young fisherman. I recalled the bayonet tearing into his flesh and the warm blood gushing onto my hands. I saw the grave I'd dug him on the beach.

"Are you alright Hilary?"

Harry Bunch grabbed my arm.

"Yes, I think so…"

"I'm so sorry sir," said the bowler-hatted man who had now caught up with his captive and was holding on to his semi-chained arms as tightly as he could – even though I sensed that the alleged 'Horrific Monster' could easily have shaken himself loose had he really wanted to. "Please accept my sincere apologies for any inconvenience caused."

As he spoke the white fur surrounding the face of the 'monster' slipped slightly revealing, for a second or two, a tantalizing glimpse of a rather more prosaic receding forehead before the bowler-hatted showman hurriedly pulled it back into position with an embarrassed smile. But the face of the young fisherman had been nothing more than an illusion. Just as much of a trick as the 'Horrific Monster' because I now reasoned that he was probably simply a conspirator in this commercial enterprise. An actor fallen on hard times I surmised. Fearful perhaps that I might declare the fraudulent nature of his business to the gathering crowd, the bowler-hatted man shot me an anxious look before dragging his hirsute and theatrically chained cohort back into the tent in an elaborate and almost comical pantomime which nevertheless had the desired effect of forcing a large percentage of the audience which had witnessed the charade to reach into their pockets, take out their pennies and form a queue outside the entrance of the tent.

12. My embarrassment is not entirely quelled.

"I DON'T KNOW what happened."

"Understandable," said Harry Bunch, regarding me thoughtfully as he puffed grey noxious fumes from his pipe. "I felt the same when I saw that poor wretch have his head hacked off in Bremen. They said it would all be done quickly and that the swordsman was the finest in the land but I swear it took more than five swipes to do the job – and each one produced a warm spurt of blood which splashed across the faces of the people in the front row. The condemned man appeared to be alive for the first two for he wriggled and screamed and moved his arms – which were bound of course – as if trying to rectify the swordsman's damage by restoring his half cut off head to its original position. I shall never forget it. And it still haunts me in my sleep to this day."

We had retired to a chop house about a hundred yards away from Newgate prison and, by the window, we had watched the thrilled and happy faces of the crowd as they walked past – some of the children playing with their hanging toys.

"At least Mr Swanston was dispatched quickly," I said.

Harry Bunch weighed up my observation in his mind.

"It's the family," he said. "They're the ones who suffer most. Death, whether it's by a blade or by a piece of rope, must be agonising for a few seconds but the pain of grief is more persistent. Mr Swanston's family were all there at the front and they'll feel it for years to come."

He blew away some fine filings from his scratch-plate and held it up to the light to inspect it. The copper caught the sun and flashed momentarily like gold. Harry Bunch, with his usual skill and artistry, had scrawled a compelling – if rather simplified – image of the condemned man dangling at the end of a noose with a priest and a hangman standing by. The crowd were represented by ever diminishing circles blending into the London skyline on the horizon – a line which was perfectly straight even though Mr Bunch had not had access to any geometrical instruments. I was reminded of Michaelangelo and his alleged ability to draw perfect circles without a compass. He blew away some more filings and wiped the plate on his sleeve before placing it down and adding a few more lines here and there for added impact.

"Why did they come?"

My companion shrugged.

"Who knows? Perhaps his mother wanted to be there at the end just as she had been at the beginning. And there's always that hope of a last-minute pardon. I suppose you heard his mother screaming out for mercy on his behalf?"

"Yes," I said. "She kept saying that she knew her boy and that he was no murderer."

"An oft-expressed appeal I fear."

"Yes, but I *believed* her Harry. Corville Swanston didn't look like a savage murderer!"

"They never do."

"But his *tears*," I said, touching his arm and stopping him from scratching the plate for an instant. "Didn't they seem genuine to you? Didn't they seem like tears of hopelessness and despair rather than remorse or guilt?"

"I've seen plenty of hangings. And, trust me, they always end up the same."

He pulled his arm away and continued adding the finishing touches to his engraving but, after shooting me some nervous glances, he sighed and pushed his plate away.

"Look," he said, "there is no shame in feeling the way you do and there's no shame either in doing what you did."

I shook my head in embarrassment at the recollection.

"Poor woman."

"You did your best to avoid her Hilary."

"Her finest frock. That's what she said."

"People throw up all the time. A public execution is a gruesome event."

He touched me gently on the shoulder.

"You'll get over it. That woman will clean up her dress and it will all be forgotten. Just look on the bright side. With The Slasher gone and Rudra recaptured the streets of London are safe again and we won't have to look at any more torn bodies."

Smiling, he resumed his engraving.

But I wasn't comforted by his well-intentioned words for they had been mis-directed. Cruel and shocking as the hanging had been, the impulse that had led me to vomit over the woman's dress had not been inspired by the events up on the gallows. Jolted by my earlier collision with the alleged 'savage' from the bowler-hatted man's tent I had been thinking of the young fisherman I had so viciously bayonetted back on the island. I had remembered his eyes as he'd stared at me in disbelief and horror. His life ebbing away as the seagulls yodelled and as the sea relentlessly crashed in.

13. The perils of Nothing are dispelled by Something.

FOLLOWING THE DEATH of The Slasher, London, like a beast that had suddenly been disturbed momentarily by a series of unexpected noises in the night, quickly went back to sleep as soon as everything became peaceful again. Naturally the fine city – as ever – bustled and rattled with the chaotic symphony of yells, screams, trundling wheels and whinnying horses; impromptu skirmishes broke out in the maze of the Seven Dials and outside some of the more disreputable taverns; harlots plied their trade by teasing, cajoling and then insulting any man who dared to pass by without succumbing to their charms; pickpockets and rogues slinked through the crowds like sharks, snipping off purses with easy success or at other times being chased and caught whilst they screamed and protested their innocence; street sellers proclaimed the freshness of their fruits, fish, pies and porter; young ladies floated elegantly in pairs along the Mall, greeting every doffed hat from passing gentlemen with aloof acknowledgement followed by a cascade of girlish giggles; the main thoroughfares became clogged with carriages, the rain hissed like bullets as they struck the hot bodies of the horses; politicians clashed; poets starved; tailors clipped; minstrels plucked. And throughout it all the Thames flowed greyly towards the sea, unmoved and unconcerned with the ephemeral comedy of human existence.

Up in his office, Mr Julius Colebridge had been heard and seen pacing around his office with his chin in his hand – his eyes apparently blind to everything except his polished shoes as they described a vague circle in the Persian rug. His secretaries knocked timidly on his door and, in response to his gruff invitation to enter, they curtseyed fearfully and placed whatever it was they'd been charged to provide – be it letters or a tray of tea – as gently as they could on the desk where, they observed, there were usually other trays or letters, unopened and undisturbed. These same secretaries, wise and perceptive as owls, were also the source of the growing concern for Mr Colebridge's general wellbeing for it had been noted how the office now smelled strongly of whiskey in the mornings and that, even though the windows had been opened, neither this pervasive odour nor the noxious one which underlay it – the unmistakeable bitterness of opium – could be eradicated. Nervous for his health, one of these secretaries approached me one morning, apologizing for the impertinence but explaining that she knew there to be a tenuous family connection between myself and Mr Colebridge. Explaining her concerns she suggested politely that I might somehow intervene. Naturally I had no recourse except to agree.

I hesitated slightly before his office door, straightened my waistcoat and turned around. The faces of the various secretaries and fellow journalists silently urged me to go ahead and so I clenched my hand into a fist and knocked. The sound on the other side was a muffled growl but I understood it to be a signal of consent so I twisted the brass doorknob and entered Mr Colebridge's office. Too my surprise he seemed sunnier than I had been led to believe and he indicated that I should take a seat, which I did.

"Do you know what I did last night Hilary? I decided to end it all."

"End it all sir?"

"All this."

He extended his arms to indicate the office.

"And all *that*."

He pointed at the window which I assumed he intended as a symbol for the world.

"But why sir?"

"Because of *nothing*!"

"I'm afraid I don't understand."

Mr Colebridge sighed and walked across to the open window.

"What do you hear?"

Like a schoolboy challenged by a question he didn't quite understand but which he knew required an immediate answer, I swallowed hard and searched for an appropriate response. None came.

"*Nothing*," snapped Mr Colebridge. "That's what you can hear boy! That's the sound of *nothing*!"

He strode back to his leather chair, swung out his coattails like a flustered raven and sat down.

"A few weeks ago those same streets were alive with talk of a mad killer and an escaped tiger."

"*Panther* sir."

"People were scared. And when people are scared do you know what that means? *Business* Hilary!"

He thumped the table with his fist.

"It means *business*."

Mr Colebridge sniffed, unfurled a handkerchief, wiped his nose delicately with it and stuffed it back in his pocket.

"Last night it was still. The moon was full and I had no desire to spend any more time pacing this office and contemplating my doom so I thought the best thing to do was to actually enable it. My doom that is. So, I took my coat, scarf and hat, locked the offices – for by then it was well past ten o'clock and I was the last one here – went out onto Piccadilly and slowly made my way down to the river. The evening was chilly but not altogether cold."

He smiled slightly and shook his head.

"It's peculiar. Whereas at first the thought of actually ending my life had filled me with what I assumed to be the customary measure of fear and trepidation, as soon as I climbed onto the side of the bridge and gazed down at the moving, stone-grey monster of the Thames, foaming and restless, all my troubles seemed to vanish as the water invited me to join it in its glorious rush towards the sea. I outstretched my arms like an eagle and prepared to take what I assumed to be my final breath but, just as I was about to tilt myself forward to accept the river's invitation salvation arrived in the most unusual form."

Mr Colebridge paused. He glanced at me and I understood it as a signal for me to cue him. I stirred in my chair.

"And what was that sir?"

"A scream."

He paused again.

"A… *scream* sir?"

"A young woman, no more than twenty, dressed in rags and drenched in what I quickly deduced to be her own blood. Hysterical, she ran up to me – as I was the only other human being on the bridge – and pulled so hard at my leg that I feared my braces would give and that at my pantaloons would collapse around my feet. Under the circumstances I decided that the best option would be to allow the Thames to continue on its journey without me for the time being whilst I addressed the concerns of this troubled young woman. It turns out that she had just been attacked by *The Slasher*!"

He paused again. A sly smile formed on his face as the old glint returned to his eye.

"But…"

"I know Hilary," he said, suddenly laughing and sitting forward again. "We *hanged* him. Or, at least, we hanged *some-one*. But whoever we hanged it wasn't The Slasher because when I followed this young woman back across the bridge I discovered that the blood on her clothes wasn't hers at all but that of her companion who now lay across the pavement in a state of tragic dismemberment. A Peeler had arrived on the scene and he was clearly as distressed as the young woman because he had thrown up all over his tunic. The body was that of the young woman's sister and it was torn and mutilated as if by the hands of the Devil himself! The Peeler pressed the hysterical girl for a description but she was in no state to talk. All she said was that the killer had pounced out of the darkness and, in a matter of seconds, her sister had been taken and the only option available to her was to run for her life."

"Forgive me," I said. "But I fail to see how this tragic event could provide any sort of salvation."

Reaching into the drawer of his desk Mr Colebridge took out a crisp copy of the latest edition of '*The Piccadilly Trumpet*'.

"*That*, my boy," he said, beaming almost manically. "Is *salvation*."

The headline of the '*Trumpet*' was bold and inescapable.

'*SLASHER STILL AT LARGE!*'

Mr Colebridge adopted a more sombre expression and shook his head.

"It seems like we hanged the wrong man, poor fellow."

But then he beamed again and, for the first time in my experience of him, raised both his feet up on the desk.

"They should never have published that false confession! So let's rub the *Trumpet's* nose in it and catch the *real* killer."

14. I am greatly surprised by another face from the past.

SO, WITH THE news that The Slasher was still on the loose, once again the dark and maze-like streets of the city were gripped by terror. Death lurked in every shadow and each sudden movement. Mr Bunch and myself were called to three sites in Westminster alone in the weeks following Mr Colebridge's encounter with the young woman on the bridge and the visions which greeted us were uniformly gruesome and entirely consistent with the murders ascribed – in vain as the whole of London now knew – to the unfortunate Corville Swanston. Buoyed by the new wave of murders and the inevitable decline of *'The 'Piccadilly Trumpet'* in the crucial areas of public opinion and trust, Mr Colebridge now entered the office each morning in neatly pressed suits, immaculately ironed shirts and with his skin as smooth as a baby's following an appointment with Mr Trumper's skilful razor. As his top hat was carefully removed the entire office could see that his sparse strands of hair had also been trimmed. This new incarnation of Mr Julius Colebridge – seemingly younger, fitter and altogether stronger – had summoned myself and Mr Harry Bunch into his office and cheerfully charged us with the recommencement of our mission to detail every single development in The Slasher – for it was definitely *he* – and to furnish the *'Gazette'* with as many lurid details as the population of London could manage, for the appetite for gore amongst the readership clearly knew no bounds and was insatiable.

One night, roughly around a month or so after Mr Colebridge's Damascene moment on Westminster Bridge, I was walking back to my lodgings in Islington along the dark and deserted streets when, ahead of me, I saw the huddled shape of a man in the doorway of a hardware shop I sometimes frequented. As I got closer I saw that he was framed by a pool of blood and that he was shifting painfully and moaning.

"Sir," I said, running up to him, bending down and extending an arm. "Let me help you sit up."

I recognized the man as the Mr Herbert Flamberry, the owner of the hardware shop, but his voice was now weak and hoarse whereas, normally, it was loud and full of cheer. The keys to his shop lay spread-eagled on the cobbles, painfully out of reach.

"Take my arm Mr Flamberry."

"I thank you sir but…it's no use. I am… done for."

"Nonsense, come. Take it."

But I saw that there was a look in Mr Flamberry's face that had gone beyond the realms of pain and into that peculiar territory of calmness which appeared to usher in the presence of Death. It was a look of almost unbearable sadness. I allowed my arm to drop to my side and we both acknowledged silently that the end was, indeed, near. As discreetly as I could I gazed down at the man's chest and belly and saw the blood gushing out almost independently of the remainder of the body, as cheerful as a geyser and making indecent trickling noises as it darkened the gaps around the cobblestones. His innards were piled up alongside him like a strange exotic plant which somehow seemed to bear no relationship at all to the gaping hole from where they had emerged.

"He was…*smaller* than I expected."

"You mustn't try to speak Mr Flamberry. And try to keep still. I will shout for help."

But as I prepared to stand up Mr Flamberry grabbed my arm, tightening his fingers with all the strength he could muster as if the words he were about to say were the most important ones he'd ever said.

"They talk of a...*giant*. He is big. But not a *giant* sir. Strong though. He is possessed of that...wiry strength you sometimes see in youths."

He grimaced in pain and released his grip.

"Let me get some help."

"They hanged the wrong man."

He once again gripped my arm.

"You must go sir! It is not safe. He only left because you approached. I hear him!"

His eyes were as large as marbles.

"*He is coming!*"

For a few seconds I wondered whether the poor man was in the hold of delirium – those final few seconds of heightened cogency before madness and confusion washed down like a wave wiping everything that had been stamped on the brain during a lifetime. I looked around me but all I saw was the empty street, the black rooftops and the cold, uncaring moon.

"*Run sir!*"

They were Mr Flamberry's final words for, in that instant, a shadow flashed from the darkness and pounced down, enveloping him and lashing out swift and deadly blows. Mr Herbert Flamberry issued one last whimper of surrender and released his soul to the mercy of the Lord. I closed my eyes tightly. I should have turned on my heels and ran as fast as I'd ever had -- screaming at the top of my voice for any kind of help for The Slasher was at my back and *thirsting for blood*! But I was trapped by some kind of invisible force which held my body like a hostage. All I could do was breathe and listen as The Slasher tore and ripped at Mr Flamberry's corpse, growling with pleasure as he did so. Finally he stopped. I imagined that his attention had now turned to me as his next victim.

"Please," I said.

It was the only word I could think of saying. But I knew it was useless. I was attempting to converse with a demon from the depths of Hell. Was this my divine punishment for killing the fisherman and leaving poor Tobias Gently at the Tower of Ectha? My throat was paper. I closed my eyes to await the agony. But then I felt something entirely unexpected. A rough tongue on the back of my hand. Loud and insistent purring. I opened my eyes and looked down.

"Mr Delphus of Clare," I said. "Is it *you?*"

15. A savage nocturnal attack!

"AH, MR DURWOOD. I've been wanting a word with you." Mrs Northcote's voice stilled me as effectively as a spear hurled into my back. I'd closed the front door to my lodgings as carefully as I could and been halfway up the stairs carrying the heavy parcel when the door to Mrs Northcote's rooms had swung open and now, when I turned around with my most innocent smile, I could see that she knew.

"Some of the others have been complaining."

She had been in the process of making one of her interminable pigeon pies because her apron was spattered with flour and she was brandishing a rolling pin like a weapon. She took a step forward and leant against the bannister.

"Mr and Mrs Clam tell me you've been buying an awful lot of meat lately."

I tried to feign innocence.

"Really?"

"Over three pounds of mutton yesterday Mrs Clam said. And two pounds of beefsteak before that. And yet I don't smell any cooking from your rooms."

The package in my hands was heavy and greasy. It was also impossible to hide.

"Nice to know someone can afford to buy so much meat. If you're that rich I dunno why you don't get yourself somewhere more fancy Mr Durwood. Buckingham Palace p'rhaps?"

I laughed nervously but she didn't reciprocate. She took another step up. The creaky one that I'd studiously avoided.

"You got a *hound* up there Mr Durwood?"

"No. Of course not." I tried to laugh it off. "The very idea."

"'Cos Mr Layton says he hears growling upstairs. Like some sort of beast. Big too he reckons."

"There's no hound Mrs Northcote. I can assure you of that."

"You knows the rules."

"Yes."

"We agreed when you moved in."

"Of course."

"No hounds."

"No."

"Or animals."

"No."

I shifted the heavy package in my arms and hoped that Mrs Northcote hadn't noticed the grease which was flowing down my arms forming dark spots on the stairs. She turned on her heel and went back into her room – slamming the door with such force that one of the cheap plaster ornaments on the hallway table rattled and toppled to the floor and smashed into several pieces. I raced up the stairs to the top of the house casting a wary eye on the door to Mr and Mrs Clam's rooms as I did so, placed the trembling key in the lock, entered, leant against the door, closed my eyes momentarily and sighed with relief.

Mr Delphus of Clare lay on the sagging settee, his long tail curled on the floor, his giant paws tucked under his chin. On seeing me he raised his head, sniffed the air, yawned – revealing his impeccable armoury of teeth, extended his deadly claws and purred.

"We must be quiet," I said, approaching him. "No one must know."

Mr Delphus of Clare thumped his head affectionately against my thigh and purred so forcefully that my jaw vibrated with his energy. He raised himself and followed me into the kitchen – the slight limp in his back leg still noticeable – as was the more recent wound which the unfortunate Corville Swanston had issued in self-defence. Watching intently as I unpacked the fresh mutton he slapped his tongue against the side of his mouth but demonstrated admirable restraint as I placed it in his bowl and sliced some of the bigger pieces into more manageable chunks. "There," I said, putting the bowl down in front of him.

Once given the command Mr Delphus of Clare devoured the fresh mutton with gusto, his purring now so loud that it almost drowned out the sound of the carriages down on the streets. I stroked the back of his head and went over to the settee and slumped down with relief.

I must have fallen asleep for the next thing I knew it was dark and the streets outside were quiet. Mr Delphus of Clare – just as he had done each night since our re-acquaintance a month or so earlier – lay beside me purring contentedly. Suddenly there was a scraping sound at the door. Someone was trying to get in. A key was turned. Mr Delphus of Clare had heard it too and he was now a big black triangle by the door, growling a warning as the scraping of the key in the lock signified that someone was making an entrance. A candle came in on a tray. Then a hand. Then an arm. I recognized the unmistakeable figure of Mrs Northcote. She was dressed in a nightgown and her cap was long, almost reaching her waist. Standing in the doorway for a few seconds she raised her tray and surveyed the room. When the flickering candlelight finally rested on the enormous figure of Mr Delphus of Clare she took a step back in fright, leaning against the wall, dropping the candle to the floor and attempting a scream which was immediately curtailed by Mr Delphus of Clare's paw as it struck her to the ground. He pounced upon her immediately, tearing instinctively at her nightgown and cap.

"*No!*"

Upon hearing my command Mr Delphus of Clare groaned to signify his reluctance but, loyal as ever, he stopped his mauling and retracted his claws. He backed away and slumped sulkily in the corner.

"Let me help you Mrs Northcote."

I helped her up to her feet and handed her the little tray where the candle, miraculously, still flickered.

"*What...is tha–*"

"Don't try to speak Mrs Northcote."

She was like a child stuck in a dream. Her nightgown was ripped down the front but I reckoned she had experienced a lucky escape for it might just as easily have been her flesh. I guided her towards the door but she was still looking over her shoulder at the growling giant cat in the shadows.

"*All I wanted was to...check th–*"

"Not a word Mrs Northcote. It's best not to speak."

Her shock and trauma expressed itself in an almost childlike obedience. She nodded as I edged her respectfully out onto the landing.

"Go to bed Mrs Northcote," I said softly. "I'll bring the rent down in the morning."

16. Another letter home.

Covent Garden,
December 15*th*.

My dear father,
  Mr Colebridge is dead. *How sad it is for me to convey this information to you in such a stark and unadorned manner but you may trust that my exhausted quill has scratched hundreds of more gentle attempts at communicating this tragic event in a more efficacious style but, in the end – and it is now almost three o'clock in the morning and I have been at my desk writing this letter since eleven – I concluded that none could emphasize the brutal fact of my benefactor's death more effectively than those four words. Forgive me father for I know that it has been a while since my last communication and my desire was not to break my silence with such an unpleasant letter. I sincerely hope that it does not have a detrimental effect on your recovery and that Mrs Bartlett will aim to comfort you shortly with one of her spicy mince pies! Mr Colebridge, I know, was a dear friend to you and you will also appreciate his great kindness to me. Not many eminent publishers would have invested money and faith in a fresh and unproven scribe who had just come down with only a modest degree and, naturally, it was not his fault that the whole venture came to a premature and unfortunate end. I blame that entirely on the shoulders of that rapscallion Mr Eustace Skate, of which more presently.*
  Father, I know that your natural curiosity will be the bane of poor Mrs Bartlett's life and upon hearing the news of your friend's demise you will bombard her with hundreds of questions which, having never even been to London, she will naturally be

unable to answer so allow me to furnish you with the unpleasant details. Mr Colebridge had, for some time, been under considerable financial strain. You will know from my previous letters that London had been in the grip of a terrifying monster called The Slasher who had preyed on some of the innocents of the city for months. Whilst clearly a menace and a danger to the general population the fear and anxiety this murderer engendered was nevertheless very profitable to the 'Gazette' and, whilst the killer stalked the streets at night – sometimes tearing a victim apart in the most vicious and degrading manner – Mr Colebridge echoed the general sense of dismay and fear whilst secretly, of course, delighting in his sales figures. Sadly for him – but joyfully for the rest of London – The Slasher has vanished. You may recall father that one unfortunate man was hanged at Newgate under the mistaken impression that he had been the killer. The Slasher returned briefly but now he has finally gone, seemingly for good. There have been no gruesome murders now for months and once more people feel safe to walk the streets at night unburdened by stick, sword, club or musket. Now, naturally, this unusual disappearance had a profound effect on poor Mr Colebridge. It is known that he had once before attempted to take his life during a previous lull in murders but now that this hiatus had proved to be more permanent, sales of the 'Gazette' plummeted and, faced with ruin, he jumped into the Thames one night and his body was swept away – later being found stuck to a tree in Southwark. His funeral was a small private affair and none but the closest family were in attendance. Sad news indeed father. In the absence of the 'Gazette' I have now joined the offices of the 'Piccadilly Trumpet'. This paper survived largely by not focusing so exclusively on The Slasher and covering various other elements of London life. I am now as their correspondent reporting on special public events. You may have read reports in The Times about the structural improvements to Old Bartholomew's Church in Aldgate? I am proud, and not a little put out it must be said, to say that they were largely based upon my original article for the 'Piccadilly Trumpet'. I have also recently been reporting on the Pineapple Fayre at the Haymarket and at the unveiling of the new statue of Lord Collingwood outside the Admiralty. Tomorrow night I venture to the famous Haberdashers Hall to cover the return of Sir Duncan Roseberry. He will recount his adventures in the South Pacific and describe his experiences at the fabled Tower of Ectha. No doubt you will have read accounts of his exploits in The Times. He will be accompanied by his friend Mr Eustace Skate whom, beforehand, will give a brief talk on his uncovering of the monastery at Pan Reng. So you will see father that, by keeping my hands busy and industrious, I have been keeping the devil at bay!

Do you remember Mr Harry Bunch? I wrote about him affectionately to you in my last letter and, indeed, he was a most allegiant – if occasionally truculent – partner. In the wake of the 'Gazette's' demise, he too has been forced onto pastures new. His skill as a draughtsman had not gone unnoticed and he too was offered a role at the 'Trumpet' but it transpires that he was tired of the documentary life and instead moved across the sea to Ireland where, I am told, he met a young lady of good family and is now engaged to be married to her. But I would not wish you to fret father or worry that I am alone and friendless now in the big city for I stumbled upon an old acquaintance of mine from my travelling adventures and we have now both settled in shared rooms in Covent Garden. Mr Delphus of Clare – for that is the name of the individual – is the most loyal creature I have ever encountered and he is also almost supernaturally protective. Why, only last night as I was venturing down to Charing Cross I was followed by a couple of men whom I swiftly deduced to be of ill-virtue and, indeed, this calculation was proved when I turned into an alley and was quickly pounced upon. One of them held a rusty knife to my breast whilst his toothless partner rummaged through my pockets for coins but, before the rascal could make good with his bounty Mr Delphus of Clare emerged from the shadows and, on seeing his fearsome demeanour and his terrifying bulk they both ran off, shrieking and screaming that they had just witnessed the coming of Satan himself! So you can see father, I am quite safe and Mr Delphus of Clare looks after me well.

The new lodgings are rather spacious and the landlord is a most liberal gentleman who cares little for his tenants' comings and goings as long as they are punctual with the rent. This compares favourably with Mrs Northcote's establishment for that lady – although initially hospitable and the creator of indisputably the finest lard cakes in the whole of London – sadly proved to be somewhat too inquisitive for her own good.

Father, my earnest hope is that I can visit you soon in Havemore Hall. I am eager to see the old place again and to sit by your bedside whilst Mrs Bartlett and Rosie bring in tea and sandwiches! I cannot say with any certainty when I shall be able to visit you father for myself and Mr Delphus of Clare have one important task to undertake before circumstances will prove favourable for such a venture. I apologize beforehand for what we must do but it has been tormenting me for years and now, finally, I feel that the power to quell these troublesome feelings that rumble like thunder within my breast is finally within my grasp.

Your loving son,
Hilary.

17. A disastrous performance.

IT SEEMED AS if the entire population of London was determined to enter Haberdashers Hall in order to see and hear the remarkable – and by now near-mythical – Sir Duncan Roseberry make his first public appearance for years. Many, of course, had assumed the worst and believed him dead. Indeed, the common jest – although nevertheless true – was that *The Times* had published his obituary twice! Many, of course, had encountered him in places such as Hyde Park, Albemarle Street, or outside the Admiralty basking in his celebrity and assuming a false modesty whenever confronted but he had so far not committed himself to a return to the public lectern. Now, tonight, he was at last ready to share his latest adventures with the world.

The long lines of excited people eager to gain admission – but surely resigned to the fact that they were unlikely to succeed – chattered like children as I strode past and presented my invitation to the stern-looking man at the door.

"From *The Piccadilly Trumpet*," I said. "Special correspondent. Hilary Durwood."

"Don't look all that special to me," said the man, looking me up and down with evident distaste before turning his head and spitting. He handed me back the card. "Squeeze in – if you can."

The invitation to the talk had arrived a few days earlier addressed to the *Trumpet*'s editor – Mr Algernon Brick – and he had succumbed to my pleas to cover the event. He was aware that I had a slight acquaintance with Mr Eustace Skate although he was unaware of the precise nature of it. So it was that I now stood in the centre of Haberdashers Hall pushed and jostled from all sides as if caught up in a particularly vicious bully. Some of the ladies were more aggressive than the men and several of them kicked me on the shin in an attempt to get closer to the stage where, in front of the drawn curtains, I could see a notice bearing the words –

'Tonight, Sir Duncan Roseberry Recounts His Tale of The Discovery of The Tower of Ectha'

Beneath it, in letters barely legible due to their relative diminutiveness, I read –

'Also, Mr Eustace Skate on the Remarkable Monastery at Pan Reng'

Cigar smoke, perfume and sweat filled the air and the roar of excited conversation was punctuated by the occasional shriek which I assumed to be attributable either to feminine delirium or to a gentleman whose foot had been almost pierced by a careless heel. The room was so full that I felt, at some point, my poor ribcage surely would soon be cracked like pastry. Looking around I saw the faces of eminent lords and ladies together with ragged-hatted tradesmen and the usual gaggle of loud youths from the Inns of Court. It appeared as if an entire representative swathe of the city was present and, indeed, it had been rumoured that the young Queen herself had insisted on coming only to be persuaded against it in the interests of decorum by her advisers. Emissaries from the palace had been sent along in her stead – or so it had been reported – with instructions to memorize and relay each word and gesture of Sir Duncan Roseberry's lecture. The notebook – which in truth I had taken along for appearances more than for utility – was swiped from my hand and lost forever in a sudden human wave as an announcer took to the stage and cleared his throat inaudibly. He waved his arms like Canute – and with a similar level of effectiveness – but, eventually, the room settled down from a roar into an expectant rumble which could be felt as much as heard. Canute waited until the hubbub had achieved acceptable levels before he cleared his throat once more, pulled at the edges of his impressive brown moustache and spoke.

"Ladies and gentlemen. I would like to welcome you all to the Haberdashers Hall tonight. I can promise you an evening of stupendous tales of adventure and death-defying events!"

At these words the room exploded like a cannon and the gentleman, visibly irritated, twiddled the edges of his brown moustache once again and frowned before raising his arms for a second time.

"Ladies and gentlemen! Please! *Please!*"

The resonating waves of the crowd were becalmed and the gentleman with the brown moustache attempted to regain his composure. He smiled professionally and extended his right arm towards the direction of the wing.

"Before Sir Duncan Roseberry's tale of high adventure on his strange and wondrous island on the far side of the globe may I please introduce you to another of our eminent gentlemen explorers who has a tale no less wondrous or no less lofty. To recall how he found and documented the lost monastery at Pan Reng please welcome *Mr Eustace Skate!*"

Despite his well-groomed appearance – he had clearly trimmed his beard and his suit and waistcoat were new and of the finest tweed – as he strode purposefully and, I concluded, rather too quickly towards the lectern, Mr Eustace Skate cut a rather unimpressive figure. The stage at the Haberdashers Hall was by no means large but it somehow served to dwarf the unfortunate fellow and this, together with the muted and rather weary applause that greeted him – petering out embarrassingly before he actually arrived at the lectern – forced me into a smile. He fumbled with his notes and I could see that his hands were shaking. One of the papers fluttered to the floor like a dying bird and Eustace Skate decided against picking it up. He looked up, smiled fearfully at the audience, cleared his throat and spoke in an uncharacteristically thin and reedy voice.

"Ladies and...gentlemen. My talk tonight is...is... based upon...my...my journey to the magnificent...the...er...wondrous monastery of...Pan Reng."

The audience began to mumble and the mumble grew to a chatter and the chatter evolved in seconds to a general hubbub which almost drowned out Mr Skate's voice. He raised it but, in doing so, only succeeded in highlighting its less than pleasing tone.

"Located deep within the…deep within the…jungles of the far east this…this…"

Helpless as a child he looked to the wings for assistance and the announcer stepped on to the stage once again and extended his arms. His voice bellowed around the room and immediately silenced it.

"Ladies and gentlemen. Please. I beg of you. I appreciate your impatience at wanting to greet Sir Duncan Roseberry back to these shores and to hear his amazing tale of how he discovered the ancient Tower of Ectha but please ladies and gentlemen, *please* give Mr Eustace Skate – a man of letters and an intrepid adventurer in his own right – the benefit of your attention while he furnishes you with his own discovery, namely the fabled monastery at Pan Ring."

"*Reng.*"

"Of course. Pan *Reng*. Forgive me."

The man with the brown moustache offered Mr Eustace Skate a bow of apology before smiling obsequiously at the audience and gliding almost soundlessly back into the wings.

Eustace Skate wiped his forehead with a handkerchief and attempted to pick up where he had left off but his notes were in disarray and I suspected that the one page he needed was the one which had dropped to the floor but which he was now too embarrassed to retrieve. Silence engulfed the Hall like smoke but gradually it was filled by more murmurs from the audience. Eustace Skate felt forced to speak. Casting a quick glance to the wings for encouragement he did so.

"Located deep in the jungle of….of….and, I mean… surrounded by ancient sculptures and…and…"

His hands were shaking like two small creatures that were entirely independent of the rest of his being and over which he had no jurisdiction whatsoever whilst the sweat now glinted in the glare of five hundred candles.

"I travelled for miles into....the...darkness of this infernal.... er...."

"Why don't you go back there?"

The man who had shouted out from the back of the room was rewarded by a wave of laughter and a smatter of applause. Up on the stage Eustace Skate tried his hardest to ignore it all but it was obvious to everyone – even himself – that his task was a thankless one and one which, sadly for him, he was also incapable of fulfilling. The moustachioed man emerged from the wings once again. He placed a sympathetic arm on the shoulder of the stunned and somewhat pale discoverer of the ancient monastery of Pan Reng, whispered something in his ear – to which Eustace Skate nodded in resigned agreement – and led him away from the lectern towards the wings to the accompaniment of some disingenuous applause.

"Bring on Sir Duncan!"

"Yes, that's who we came to see!"

I greeted the pain of Mr Eustace Skate as a form of divine retribution. I smiled. But if my plan succeeded, it would be as nothing to the pain he would shortly experience.

18. *A most scandalous misrepresentation of the Tower of Ectha.*

" A *PLAIN.* THAT is what I would like you to imagine ladies and gentlemen! A featureless expanse extending for hundreds, nay, thousands of miles! No tree or bush to relieve the monotony. Only sand and stone and rock. The wind is King here. Commander and sovereign. The wind decides the shape and contours of the landscape. The wind creates ripples and dunes. The wind attempts to repel all invaders and that is why it throws up clouds of dust into my face. *My face* ladies and gentlemen! The first human visage to enter this forsaken region for *a full millennium!*"

The audience gasped as one. But then Haberdashers Hall settled into complete and utter silence again as, up on the stage, Sir Duncan Roseberry carefully poured some water from a jug into his glass and took a rejuvenating sip, swilling the liquid around his mouth and swallowing with a fleshy croak that could be heard even at the back of the room. He paused as expertly as a Shakespearian actor, examining the faces in the crowd, then narrowing his eyes and extending his arm slowly towards them – lowering his voice as he stepped away from the lectern.

"Imagine this plain, ladies and gentlemen. Imagine being a prisoner to its barrenness. Imagine wondering if you would ever again see a human face or hear God's own tongue being spoken. As my feet trudged wearily across the sand and rocks – my eyes trained hopelessly on the cruel horizon – that is what I imagined. A desolate and lonely end to my wretched existence, my body collapsing in a bony heap to be pecked at and eventually picked clean by the voracious vultures which circled above me coming ever closer. *Ever lower with each step I took.*"

A lady next to me gasped and tugged the arm of her gentleman companion. Her eyes were wide and tearful. Aware that every face in the room was trained on him and that his words had the power of a cavalry division, Sir Duncan Roseberry performed a slight smile and shook his head as if the memory of the events he was retelling had struck him for the first time. He returned to the lectern – at exactly the point at which he had rehearsed it – in order to give the impression that his private moment of reflection was over.

"But then ladies and gentlemen...*salvation*. A most peculiar form of salvation I happily admit and not one that I would ever have expected to engender such joy or hope in a simple Englishman's heart but salvation it was and it came in the shape of a spire. Yes ladies and gentlemen. A *spire*. We see hundreds of them every day as we negotiate the streets of this fine city and we never give them a moment's thought or reflection but let me tell you ladies and gentlemen, a spire *signifies* something. A spire signifies civilization. Ever since man emerged from the primordial swamp and left the caves in his fur and bare feet he entertained the notion of creating a legacy, something to demonstrate to the world that he had existed and that this existence was not one that had been constrained or dominated by the mundane necessities of mere survival. No, he wanted to show future generations that he had sought spiritual sustenance too and that is why he and hundreds of others gathered together stones and rocks and formed them into mounds. Gradually, as man became more expert in these matters the mounds became spires and towers. That is what I saw piercing the horizon that day ladies and gentlemen. Not the tip of a simple architectural edifice. No. What I saw was the promise of *civilization!*"

The lady next to me gasped again. There were tears streaming down her face and she was still clinging on to the arm of her gentleman as if it was the only thing stopping her from drifting up to the ceiling in a state of rapture. Sir Duncan Roseberry stroked his beard. Then he glanced up at the audience as though he had only just noticed that he had company. He smiled, took a deep breath and continued.

"I walked towards it ladies and gentlemen," he said, lowering his voice but aware that – owing to the near complete silence in the hall – he was still perfectly audible to everyone. "My weary feet bloodied and stripped of flesh, my face whipped by the wind, my hair and beard long and unruly and caked with sand and dead flying insects. And the closer I got the more I realized that this was no ordinary tower. I stood and tried to assess its height but, ladies and gentlemen, my neck would not allow my head to bend back far enough in order to see the summit of this incredible structure. I swiftly deduced that the Tower of Babel itself would have been a mere bagatelle if it had suddenly been resurrected to its full glory and placed alongside this edifice. And that's when I knew, ladies and gentlemen, that I was standing in front of the famed... *Tower of Ectha.*"

As he had fully expected, the audience gasped and applauded. He smiled and raised his voice.

"Famed in mythology as one of the neglected wonders of the ancient world – in fact its very existence was held in doubt by many eminent scholars – here, ladies and gentlemen, in hard stone and block, held together by doughty mortar, stood the building which had served as the Holy Grail for all explorers and adventurers since the very beginning of time! I fell to my knees! The tears ran down my cheeks and I looked to the heavens. Clenching my hands in prayer I thanked the Lord for delivering me to its proximity and then I stood up and ran towards the tower, running my hands over the stones and rocks, feeling the roughness, scraping my thumbs along the crumbling mortar and rubbing it into my beard for I was delirious! Driven into a state of frenzy by the long days and nights in the desert and now standing at the very gates of delirium in my joy at having discovered the ancient tower. What did it look like? A very clear and honest question which I am sure I on all your lips. Allow me ladies and gentlemen..."

Sir Duncan Roseberry turned to the wings and gave a signal. Immediately, the brown moustachioed man scampered out holding a blackboard on which had been pinned some sheets of paper. The audience inside the hall murmured in excited anticipation as the moustachioed man carefully placed the blackboard next to the lectern and scampered off again with the agility of a ballerina. Sir Duncan Roseberry stepped up to the blackboard.

"Denuded as I was of all worldly possessions save the rags I wore on my back I was unable to record the wondrous tower at the time in words or pictures but I stamped the vision and the impressions in my mind and protected them with as much intensity as if they were our young Queen's finest jewels. I made a promise to unburden myself of this precious cargo as soon as I reached civilization and secured for myself a pen and paper. This I did upon arriving at the port of Xing Lei soon after my rescue. Forgive my rude and inept scribblings ladies and gentlemen but, in my defence, this drawing and all the others I will show you this evening were devised swiftly and under the most pressing of circumstances. Plagued by devilish mosquitoes and pressed by the inordinate heat and thin air of that notorious port my mission was to communicate with as much accuracy as I could muster the wonders of the ancient tower on that faraway island and so these modest creations were scraped together on these rough sheets by quill and whatever ink I could find."

The audience protested at such modesty and expressed it by all shouting at once so that the great explorer could be in no doubt that he was, in fact, a draughtsman easily the equal of a Rembrandt or Reynolds. Pleased with the predictable results of his well-practised humility, Sir Duncan smiled and bowed to express his appreciation and this gesture engendered a sponta-neous crash of wild applause and cheers. With a swish of his cape – and whilst the applause still raged – Sir Duncan turned back to the blackboard and quickly flicked through some more examples of fine draughtsmanship. Each picture presented a different aspect of the tower – from the east, west, close up and distant and I suspected darkly that these imaginative creations had been commissioned by Sir Duncan anonymously from some poor but promising young student. Sir Duncan Roseberry raised his hands and quelled the applause.

"So you see ladies and gentlemen, even by virtue of my undexterous efforts, the Tower of Ectha still stands. Taller than a mountain and just as strong after thousands of years there are turrets and windows and wooden doors larger than those fronting our famous Abbey. Let those who tell you that it is merely a myth – or, worse, a jumbled and neglected pile of rubble – let them know that you have seen these pictures ladies and gentlemen. Let them know that you have heard my description. Let them know that you have heard how an ordinary Englishman armed with nothing more than determination, conviction and, yes it must be conceded, a certain obstinance, saw it with his own eyes…"

A gasp from the audience.

"…felt the stones with his own hands…"

Another gasp.

"…closed his eyes and virtually heard the voices of the ancient Ecthans all around him…"

More gasps.

Sir Duncan Roseberry sighed and affected an impression of humbleness.

"Of course you may insist that my lecture here tonight is a mere fiction."

"*We believe you sir!*" shouted a man in front of me.

"*And me!*"

"*Me too!*"

Soon the various shouts became a chorus of support.

"Please," he said, calming the room with his arms. "I appreciate your demonstration of faith. But you will be as aware as I am that we live in an age of doubt and cynicism. We live in an age where tales of wonder and adventure are treated with derision. We live in an age, ladies and gentlemen, where our small and everyday lives and concerns – important as they are – are in danger of eradicating the spirit of curiosity which sparks the urge to travel and discover as my distinguished colleague Mr Eustace Skate and your humble servant have done in order to furnish you with a glimpse of that other, more magical world. Now, you will doubtlessly want to hear how I escaped from the island, how I found the shore and hailed down a passing galleon to Portugal."

He leant forward and lowered his voice, winking mischievously.

"But that, ladies and gentlemen, will be a tale for another day. Goodnight."

With another swish of his cape and to the roar of cheers, applause and stamping feet, Sir Duncan Roseberry left the lectern and the very walls of Haberdashers Hall seemed to be quaking with the noise. I looked up and the chandeliers were swinging and rocking perilously. A final wave and Sir Duncan Roseberry disappeared, basking in the love and admiration of every person in the room.

All except one.

19. I am finally avenged.

"THE FIRST CASUALTY of any good tale my dear Skate, is the truth. The truth is no good to a wily storyteller. No, to him, the truth is nothing but a hindrance – something wilful, intractable and pertinacious. Like a rocky coast would be to a sailor. Or a castle wall to a horseman. For you see my dear fellow, the truth is immoveable and undisputable and so we must avoid it at all costs and adapt it to suit our needs. Because the tale always come first. Everything else in our armoury – be it our vocabulary, gestures or whatever skills we might possess as actors – must always serve that insatiable urge by an audience to know what happened next."

Eustace Skate walked alongside Sir Duncan Roseberry on the quiet alleyway like a young Oppidan with his head bowed.

"Perhaps that is where I failed," he said despondently. "I have no gift for acting and a somewhat limited palette when it comes to words."

Sir Duncan Roseberry stopped in his tracks and placed his arm on his companion's shoulder.

"My dear fellow," he said. "Those things can be developed over time. I have at least ten years advantage over you in the art of storytelling. When I began I felt that I was incapable of fulfilling my destiny too. But it will come my dear Skate. Fret not about that. It will come."

They both continued walking again.

"No Skate," said Sir Duncan Roseberry after taking a few steps, "your mistake tonight was in serving empirical truth too rigidly and forgetting that other truth – the magical one which is universal and unfettered. The truth that speaks to the hearts of men and women. Hearing of how a young Arthur unsheathed a

sword from a stone when other – much stronger – men had failed
makes us realize the probable element of fantasy in the episode
but, nevertheless, it speaks a truth to us which is deeper than any
detailed description of a long-forgotten monastery deep in the
jungles of the orient. *Hush!*"

Sir Duncan Roseberry stopped again. He looked behind him.
"Are we being followed?"

Eustace Skate had stopped too. Indeed, Sir Duncan's arm had
barred any prospect of further progress on his part.

"*Followed?*"

"Listen."

In the darkness I clung to the shadows like a scorpion. I
clutched the hilt of the bread knife I had stuffed into my belt
before leaving my lodgings for Haberdashers Hall and now it
was slippery with sweat.

"I hear nothing sir."

Sir Duncan Roseberry was sceptical. He peered directly into
the darkness – directly at me. But I was clouded in shadows. I
dared not even breathe. Somewhere in the distance a dog barked.
It was answered by another even further. From the main thorough-
fare a few streets away I heard the rattle and clatter of a late-night
carriage. With every elongated second I wondered whether I
should run. My plan was foolish. *I was an idiot!* Murdering Sir
Duncan Roseberry and Eustace Skate was a deranged and sense-
less scheme conjured out of rage and pride! As I pressed my back
as far as it would go against the brickwork I wondered whether the
best plan would be to forget revenge and leave Sir Duncan Roseberry to his empty fame and glory. Eustace Skate too. What had
happened back in Singapore and on the island suddenly felt like
an event from someone else's life. Something that had happened a
hundred years earlier. Something of no real importance.

"I think we may have lost the last of the stragglers sir," said
Eustace Skate carefully. "Emerging out of the side door whilst
the waiting crowd was distracted by a fine coach was a stroke

of genius if I may say so. As was this somewhat obscure route which, although slightly malodourous and convoluted, has served us well."

Sir Duncan Roseberry emitted a low growl of discomfort and suspicion. But then he dropped his arm from his companion's chest.

"My wariness is perhaps a symptom of age," he said. "And of my fame of course. We may have travelled the world and found ourselves in all manner of tight corners but we sometimes forget, my dear Skate, that the streets and alleyways of this great city can often be more treacherous than the densest jungle. But come. I know a good tavern not far from this vicinity which serves a fine cognac and where we will be unmolested."

They walked away and I waited a few seconds for my heart to stop pounding and to allow myself a deep breath. My body sagged forwards like one that had just ran a full mile across rugged terrain but, as the warm hilt of the bread knife pressed into my belly I realized that I had to move otherwise I would lose my quarry in the unfamiliar, labyrinthine alleys. So, still keeping to the shadows as much as I could – and trying to make my feet travel as soundlessly as possible across the dried mud and stones – I resumed my pursuit and continued for a few yards until I tripped over a raised slab and was sent crashing to the ground. Ahead of me I heard Sir Duncan's bellowing voice.

"Who's there? Reveal yourself or be damned!"

I picked myself up from the ground and realized that my only option was to turn and run but before I could do so Sir Duncan Roseberry approached and was standing less than ten yards away. Instinctively I swiped the bread knife from my belt and adopted an aggressive stance in the hope that it would mask my latent fear but Sir Duncan Roseberry wasn't fooled. He studied the tremulous blade and broke into a smile. Then he laughed.

"And what do you plan to do with that sir? Slit my jugular? Take my purse?"

He took a step forward and pulled down his collar exposing his throat.

"Do your worst my good man. One quick strike and I shall slip off this mortal coil and your night's work will be done."

Feigning annoyance that I had not done as he had commanded he frowned and raised his voice.

"Well come on man! If you're going to brandish a knife then at least have the decency to use it!"

Confusion and fear swam around my head like a shoal of startled fish in the presence of a shark. I lunged half-heartedly at Sir Duncan's midriff but he stepped back and drew his pistol. Cocking it, he pointed it at my head and I stared down the barrel imagining the ball waiting patiently to be dispatched to its new home in my warm and malleable brain. I dropped the knife to the ground and raised my hands in surrender.

"Killing you is entirely legal under the circumstances," said Sir Duncan, studying me with his one eye as if I was nothing more than an inanimate target. "I could claim, quite reasonably, that I was acting in self-defence. No court in the land would convict me. That's one of the advantages of fame you see. I would elicit the sympathy and admiration of any jury and, besides, I have a credible witness here in the shape of my good friend Mr Eustace Skate."

During Sir Duncan's speech I had gazed down the barrel of his gun. It was unnervingly steady without the merest trace of nervousness. One finger was all that separated me from sudden pain and subsequent oblivion. It could just as easily be activated by accident as design for the ground was unsteady and the trigger all too sensitive to pressure.

"Why, I do believe I…*recognize* this fellow," said Eustace Skate.

"You do?"

"Yes. Step forward a little into the light."

Hesitatingly I obeyed Eustace Skate's command. Eustace Skate examined me as if I was an interesting scientific specimen.

He looked up and down before walking around like a farmer at market. Then he stood in front of me again.

"By Jove," said Sir Duncan Roseberry, dropping his pistol to his side and stroking his beard. "I do believe you're right Skate! There *is* something vaguely familiar about his face."

I reached into my pocket and took out the crumpled flower I had been given back at the tower. Cradling the delicate dead petals carefully in my hand I gave it to Sir Duncan Roseberry. As he looked at it his demeanour changed from one of effortless authority and confidence to one of shock. He looked directly into my eyes and I detected a sense of fear in him.

"*Durflap?*"

"You left me to die," I said. "And you also Mr Skate. You both abandoned me in order to pursue your own glories. I was a young man. Naïve and trusting. A young man who admired you both and you took advantage of this. Because of your actions I should either be a jumble of bones resting at the bottom of the ocean and picked clean by fish or a pitiful skeleton at the base of a pile of rocks on a desolate island untouched by civilized hands."

"My dear fellow…"

Sir Duncan Roseberry laughed and extended his hand in greeting but I shunned it.

"If anyone here is a robber or a thief," I said, my voice sounding tremulous and weedy to my ears. "It was *you* gentlemen. You robbed me of my faith, ambition and dreams. By rights both of you should be standing in the dock at the Old Bailey charged with heinous crimes but, sadly, men of your fame and standing always find a friend in the law. Which is why, tonight, I have sought a more direct form of justice."

I quickly picked up the knife and held it up to Sir Duncan Roseberry's throat.

"Drop your pistol."

He did so.

I pressed the blade against his throat and I saw his Adam's apple bob in panic.

"*Don't be a fool Durflong!*"

The blade was sharp and jagged. Because of the bobbing Adam's apple it inadvertently nicked the skin and drew blood.

"*You'll hang!*"

"Try not to speak Sir Duncan."

"How on earth did you get back?"

As he spoke the jagged blade sliced further into his skin.

"By the same means as yourself sir. A naïve young fool took my place and I reached the coast and eventually drew the attention of a clipper."

"We have...so much...in...*common* Durflight..."

"Sir, the more you speak the more this blade –"

"Perhaps we should...discuss this...over a glass of cognac...we could –"

"Sir, I can't emphasize it enough. It really would be of considerable advantage to yourself if, under the circumstances, you resisted the urge to speak."

Warm blood from the cuts on his throat turned his beard dark red. The warm liquid trickled down the blade of the bread knife, along the hilt and down my hand. I had wrongly assumed that Eustace Skate had stepped back into the shadows out of his characteristic cowardice but I quickly realized that I had been mistaken for he now ran up to me, grabbed my knife arm, twisted it around my neck and hurled me face-first into the cobblestones. I heard the knife clatter away uselessly.

"Excellent work Skate!"

"Something I picked up from the monks in Pan Reng," he said, sitting on my back – his knees digging into my spine as he pulled back my arms until I was convinced they would snap like saplings. "An ancient form of wrestling which they developed to defend themselves against the local bandits. I became quite proficient at it during my time."

"That, sir, is plain to see," said a delighted Sir Duncan Rose-berry.

From my lopsided vantage point, with the cobblestones pressing into my cheek, I saw him inspecting the blood on his beard and tapping the cuts on his neck with his fingertips.

"Those monks were peaceful and pliant," said Eustace Skate. "But once roused or threatened they became as dangerous as any wild beast of the forest. On one memorable occasion I witnessed a thief having his head ripped off his shoulders in one swift move. *Like this –*"

Eustace Skate tugged my hair and pulled back my head to the very extremes of skeletal endurance.

"Best let him go Skate."

"But I was keen to demonstrate sir."

"I realize that but –"

"They pulled back the head *like so…*"

I tried to scream but my throat was impacted.

"…and then, in a flash, they wrenched it *like this* and –"

His words were interrupted by a loud roar. I felt Eustace Skate's weight lift from my back as if it had been whipped up by a giant hand. My head, free again, hit the cobblestones with a thud but I scrambled into the shadows as I witnessed Mr Delphus of Clare dragging Eustace Skate away as if he was nothing but a pile of rags. He ripped into his belly with his claws and I watched breathlessly as Eustace Skate's entrails erupted in a fountain of blood – pink, grey and flapping like obscene snakes, they were squelched beneath Mr Delphus of Clare's giant back paws. The sound of tearing flesh was punctuated by Eustace Skate's ever weakening screams and guttural groans of protest. His dismembered hand – its fingers still clawing desperately against the empty air – skidded across the cobblestones. Finally, the screams stopped. They were replaced by a sickening wrench and an ominous snap. A hot stripe of blood splashed along my cheeks and Mr Eustace Skate's severed head rumbled by as unevenly as a rugger ball – his face frozen forever in a mixed expression of terror and surprise.

Having dispatched one of my attackers, the enormous cat turned its attention to Sir Duncan Roseberry who, by now, had collapsed like a terrified child against a wall and was sobbing, trying to make himself as small and as insignificant a proposition for the snarling beast in front of him.

"There's a...*good fellow*..."

Mr Delphus of Clare growled and took a few steps towards him – strands of Eustace Skate's bloody skin and hair still stuck to his claws. Sir Duncan Roseberry kicked his legs in a vain effort to push himself further up against the wall. I noticed a dark pool forming beneath him, steaming in the cold night air.

"...*good cat....nice cat*..."

I scrambled slowly to my feet and, for a second, Mr Delphus of Clare halted his advance towards his cowering victim and turned his head to me as if for further orders. Receiving no indication that he should stop he purred and the cobblestones seemed to vibrate.

"Durfleep, is this...animal *yours?*"

"I doubt whether any man could claim ownership of his soul sir."

"But...but...he seems to...have a certain *attachment?*"

"It's true we survived a great adventure. I must admit I thought he had perished. But he is hardy and determined. Perhaps he swam. Perhaps he too was rescued. We shall never know."

"That business back on the island," said Sir Duncan Roseberry, trying again to smile. "It was simply... *a misunderstanding*. My plan all along was to reach the shore and alert any passing ship of your predicament! When I was eventually spotted I did just that but the crew were Portuguese and *spoke no English*! I gestured and I protested as best I could but my impression was that the captain was *in a hurry*! He had doubtlessly heard of the island's dangerous reputation and had only stopped out of necessity for fresh water! We rowed back to the clipper and were gone in *less than an hour! There was nothing I could do! Surely you can see that?*"

Mr Delphus of Clare growled. He studied his prey with gleeful anticipation, the drool silver and viscous, glinting in the moonlight.

Sir Duncan Roseberry swallowed hard.

"Save me," he pleaded. "Save me from this...*thing!* This... *infernal demon from Hell!* I beg you man! I'll give you anything. Save me. *Please Durwood!*"

"Finally," I said. "You have remembered my name."

I picked up his discarded pistol, cocked it, pointed it directly at his head and pulled the trigger. The ball entered his forehead with a crack and left a perfect red circle. Sir Duncan Roseberry's face froze momentarily. Then he slumped forward with a sigh of capitulation as the gushing blood turned the pool black. Behind me I heard the sound of rushing feet and whistles. I stroked Mr Delphus of Clare's enormous head and he purred contentedly. I dropped the pistol to the ground and raised my arms in surrender. A bird fluttered down from the heavens, settling on my shoulder.

20. A final letter home.

January 12th.
Newgate Prison.

My dearest father,
How tormented must your poor soul be at my current predicament! I can only apologize yet again, in retrospect of my terrible actions, as I did in my previous letter in advance of them. For yes father, you have – through no fault of your own – spawned a cold-hearted murderer. A cold-hearted murderer who shot and killed the great Sir Duncan Roseberry – 'in cold blood' as the sensationalist news sheets would have it – and who, as a result of this crime, is now the most hated man in England having deprived the nation of one of its most prominent heroes. Even our young Queen, I am told, is almost blind with fury at such an outrage and there are rumours that she will be here in the morning incognito to watch me hang and to cheer with joy along with her unsuspecting subjects.
Father, I did shoot Sir Duncan. Of that there is no doubt. As I registered my guilty plea in front of the court having sworn to tell the truth, the whole truth and nothing but the truth or otherwise face God's wrath I was willing to confess that, on that fateful night following the lecture at Haberdashers Hall, I had raised Sir Duncan Roseberry's own pistol. I had squeezed his own trigger. And I had released his own ball into the middle of his own brain. Of that there was, and is, no dispute. And yet my conscience is strangely clear in this matter for – as you will learn after you have read the full confession – did he not himself leave me to rot and die on that cursed island? In avenging myself of his cruelty and selfishness was I not

somehow vindicated? I cannot feel sorry for the gentleman's demise father, any more than I can feel sorrow for the savage fate that befell Mr Eustace Skate. That, of course, was not a crime which could be attributed to me and Mr Delphus of Clare was apprehended for it. No doubt he would have torn the Peelers to shreds had I not commanded him to quell his growling and surrender. Having hanged one innocent man in the process they were convinced that they had now finally found their Slasher and they dragged the pliant creature away on a pole having secured his deadly paws in two separate sets of cuffs. Two weeks ago, in front of a crowd of thousands – as I am sure you will have read in The Times – they hanged him. He met the end with dignity and courage. Poor old Mr Delphus of Clare. He had lived a hard life of adventure and close shaves and now he became the first – and possibly last – cat to be publicly executed in England.

So, my loyal and – admittedly – savage companion is gone and I am alone in my cell. It has been two months since the trial and my execution has been stayed for so long that some of the editorials in the newspapers – again as you will have seen – have frothed and spat with naked fury at delay after delay when the whole of London is eager to see me hang. The reason, I am told, for this prevarication is because the sheer size of the crowds they anticipate has required the acquisition of larger stretches of land to accommodate the bloodthirsty throng. It has worked to my favour however. You may assume that this is because I am clinging on to each last second of my existence with all the desperation I can muster but the truth is that I have been given the not insignificant sum of seven hundred and fifty guineas to write my confession by Mr Algernon Brick, the owner and editor of the 'Piccadilly Trumpet'. His intention is to serialize them in his scurrilous organ and then, when I am gone, to publish them as a leather-bound volume for wider distribution and posterity. It is quite ironic, father, that I am finally to be a successful author but only after I myself will cease to be around to savour the spoils of my fame! Such are the vagaries and cruelties of life.

Father, I would not have undertaken this venture if I did not seek to make amends and to explain fully to you the nature of the events which led to my current situation. Of all my future readers you will be the most important to me and my one condition on accepting Mr Brick's offer was that you could read the entire manuscript before it was published. When it arrives by special courier at Havemore Hall – together with this, my final letter to you – I can only hope that you will read it and come to an understanding, at least, of what happened. I have also instructed Mr Brick to send you the seven hundred and fifty guineas and I am sure that it will be of use in mending the guttering or the deteriorating chimneys which you always appear to be troubled by. Mr Brick also requested if you might be willing to allow him to reproduce some of the letters I sent you over the years – including the one which miraculously eventually reached you by bottle – in order to punctuate the narrative of my confession. It is, of course, entirely up to you should you wish to comply with this.

I am prepared to die because I deserve it. Not so much for the murder of Sir Duncan Roseberry – which is the principal reason for my fate – but for that of two others for whom I feel nothing but the utmost guilt and shame. Nightly, father, I think of the poor fisherman I killed back on the island and I am equally tormented in my nightmares by the innocent and trusting face of Tobias Gently whom I left to die back at the Tower of Ectha. For these deaths I deserve to hang. You will learn of them father when you read the confession. I can only beg for your forgiveness.

Forgive me also for the hurried nature of my writing towards the final stages. The knocking and clacking of the carpenters as they construct the gallows where I will shortly hang dictated the speed at which I attempted to complete my task. Had I been a gentleman of leisure with all the time in the world at his command no doubt the prose would have been more elegant but I was eager to present the full story and to provide a complete picture of what happened in my short, but eventful life.

I shall miss you father. I shall miss Havemore Hall. I shall miss the smell of the meadow and the wet bark. I shall miss visiting Old Jacob's grave. In this parcel father you will find a pressed flower in an envelope. It is not particularly pretty or well-preserved but I should be grateful if you could instruct the new man to place it upon Old Jacob's headstone. The wind may claim it but no matter. Had he not inspired me all those years ago with his dented globe in the stable then, who knows, I might today be a free man – but I would not be so wise.

I love you father and I want you not to grieve for me unduly. I am prepared for my death and I am told that it will happen either tomorrow morning or the day after. Do not come father. And do not send Mrs Bartlett or Rosie or the new man as representatives. People will hurl rotting vegetables and fruit at me and I should not wish you to be caught in the maelstrom. They will swear and cuss and raise their fists in anger and I shall die with the vengeful swirl of hatred spinning around my head. But it shall be but a moment father. Simply a moment. And then the silence. Impenetrable and absolute.